CW00497504

Murder at the Vicarage: A Jessie Harper Paranormal Cozy Mystery

A Jessie Harper Paranormal Cozy Mystery, Volume 1

KJ Cornwall

Published by Hendry Publishing, 2023.

MURDER AT THE VICARAGE: A JESSIE HARPER PARANORMAL COZY MYSTERY

First edition. August 31, 2023.

Copyright © 2023 KJ Cornwall.

ISBN: 979-8223789710

Written by KJ Cornwall.

Table of Contents

Prologue

IN THE YEAR 1936, LIVERPOOL, England was marked by the Great Depression, causing unemployment, poverty, and a rise in crime. Despite this, the city was bustling with life. Women could be seen wearing the fashions of the day, cloche hats and velvet coats, walking down the streets with small umbrellas shielding their faces. To the keen observer, they could be seen dodging the occasional group of noisy dockers laughing and moving in and out of pubs not knowing if any man would find work again tomorrow. Those dockers and many other citizens demonstrated the never-say-die attitude that was prevalent throughout the city. Liverpool is a city of contrasts. Thousands upon thousands of men worked as dockers on the eight-mile stretch of dock land running from the north to the south of the city. Their work brought previously unimagined prosperity to the city, to such an extent that by 1914 Liverpool had more millionaires living within its boundaries than any other city in the British Empire apart from London.

But for the majority of dockworkers, particularly in the early part of the 20th century, this newfound prosperity was not some-thing that they could share in. Crammed into crumbling tenement houses in the streets that flanked the docks where they worked, their existence was anything but glamorous as they went from one day to the next wondering if they would find work thanks to the system of casual labour that left them lining up in pens like cattle hoping to be picked out for a day's work by the foreman. The situation was so bad in the 1930s that a future government foreign secretary was moved to describe the dock road as "the nearest thing to slave pens in Western civilisation."

Despite hardships, most folks did their utmost to make life as cozy, they might say comfy, as possible in their tightly knit communities. Never forget a city is merely a collection of villages and the people who live in these villages are bound together by the same institutions as those isolated places out in the countryside, namely the churches and the pubs. The former instilled the fear of God into the young and then when they were older, the latter became the fount of all knowledge to the uneducated. The combined effect was that if one believed in God and an afterlife, which many did, wasn't it conceivable there was a devil and much evil in the world. Let's call it the supernatural world so as not to frighten the children.

Chapter 1

JESSIE HARPER IS ALONE in her room in the boarding house in the Sefton Park area of Liverpool. It's run by a grumpy old spinster called Mrs Rimmer. No one knows if Mrs Rimmer has a first name. She's just simple Mrs Rimmer. Jessie is sitting on her bed and talking to her cat, a fine sleek black feline with green eyes who purrs at hearing her voice. "Khan, you do know we have to live somewhere else. Mrs Rimmer has decided she hates cats." Khan rubbed up against her arm as if to reassure her all will be fine. "I think it's an excuse to rent my room out to someone who will pay more," Jessie said, "but it gets worse. My temporary contract at the Picton Reading Room is about to expire and they won't be renewing it either there or at the Hornby Library."

Khan said, "As for Mrs Rimmer, it is an excuse. I heard her talking to the postman and she admitted as much. Sorry to hear you are to lose your job."

"I knew it." Jessie said, "Now, Khan, it's more important than ever that no one suspects you can talk or that I can hear you. Some bigots may say I'm a witch and we can't be having that now, can we? No, don't answer."

"Don't worry, "Khan said, "I know if other humans are around. Do you remember the first time you heard me talk?"

"The first or second time?" Jessie said.

"Oh, okay then miss smarty pants. It was the second time. The first was when I shocked you in the library and I swore I wouldn't talk again."

"Yes, but tell me again. I love this story," Jessie said.

"You were sat on the sofa, enjoying a quiet evening at home. Suddenly, you heard a voice behind you. 'Hey, Jessie. How's it going?' You turned around to see me staring back at you with wide, curious eyes."

'Did you just talk?" You asked, startled.

"Sure did," I replied. "Don't worry, it's not as strange as it seems." Understandably you looked confused, scared even. I knew you were thinking, how was it possible for my cat to talk? And why was I the only one who could hear him?

"What's going on?" you asked.

I jumped up onto the sofa next to you and settled myself comfortably. "Well, it's kind of complicated," I said. "But long story short, I've been given the ability to communicate with you. And you're the only human who can hear me unless we say otherwise."

I could see your mind racing. "Who gave you this ability?" you asked.

I looked away because I wasn't sure how you would react. "Let's just say I have some connections in high places," I said cryptically. "And as for why you can hear me, it's because you have a special gift. You're in tune with the supernatural world in a way that most humans aren't."

"But why me?" you asked.

Then I purred contentedly. "Because you're kind and caring, and you've always treated me with love and respect. And now, I want to repay you by helping you. You see, Jessie, there are dark forces at work in the world. Forces that humans can't even begin to comprehend. But I can see them, and I can help you navigate through them."

"Yes, I was intrigued. I had always been fascinated by the supernatural. After all, that was my section in the library, and the thought of having a talking cat as my guide was both exciting and terrifying," you said.

"Yes, then you asked, 'What kind of dark forces are you talking about?'"

I sighed. "The kind that prey on humans. The kind that use their powers to manipulate and control. But with my help, we can protect ourselves and those we care about. We can be a force for good in this world. You then looked at me with a newfound respect. I think you had always known that I was special, but no one, not even you, never could have imagined this.

'Okay,' you said. 'I'm in.' After that, you explained to me how you gave me the name Khan and that made me realise you definitely thought I was special. I mean you could have called me Fred, Joe, Tiddles, even Marmaduke," and with that I grinned just like the Cheshire Cat.

"I told George the reason I called you Khan and he was impressed too."

"Good," Khan said, "but where are we going to live once Mrs Rimmer says we have to go?"

"George has asked me if I will join him in his new business."

"How will that help find us a room?" Khan muttered.

"Patience, my friend, I will get to that."

"Sorry," Khan said.

"George's new business is a private detective agency. He has an office in Dale Street not far from the Town Hall and the Main Bridewell. The rent also includes a flat with two bedrooms, kitchen and living room. George has asked me if I'm interested in becoming his business partner and if so, I can have one of the two bedrooms."

"What are you waiting for?" It sounds purrfect."

"Quit those jokes, now, Khan." Jessie said grinning.

Khan nodded. "Okay, no more jokes. Good. We have work to do."

"We do but first let's lay down some rules." Jessie said.

"Why? I am house trained."

"Not those kinds of rules, silly, rules about your invisibility and other powers when George is around," Jessie said.

"That's easy enough. I will always seek your permission if I want to talk to you and George could overhear, and I will warn you beforehand if I go into my 'now-you-see-me-now-you-don't mode.' How's about that?"

"You are funny, yes, that's fine. And you MUST warn me if you are going into mutating mode."

"Meowtating?"

"No, you know how you love to play pranks on unsuspecting humans. One moment you can be a book on the shelf, and the next, it's a teacup on the table. Your mischievous nature keeps everyone guessing and laughing. But that sort of thing could spell big trouble for me."

"Spell... as in witch?"

"Precisely, and I'm not so don't do it unless I say it's okay, right?"

"Got it."

And with that, the unlikely duo made a solemn pact to uncover the secrets of the supernatural world; to protect those they loved from the forces of darkness, and help George succeed with the detective agency.

Chapter 2

THE NEW OFFICE IS A rented room in a small street just off Dale Street and close to the Main Bridewell, the police lock-up. Space is at a premium, small, cramped and sparsely decorated. Two desks with matching chairs, two more chairs, but mismatched and waiting hopefully for new clients, a filing cabinet bereft of files also join with the chairs waiting for clients, a coat rack and a map of the city pinned to the wall. A small windowless stock room doubles as a kitchen with a sink and kettle. There is some shelving for the tea, sugar, a bottle of evaporated milk, some cracked plates, cups, and a motley mix of cutlery. George Jenkins sits alone in the office on the one of the two chairs behind his desk. He puts his cup of tea down and shivers. The weather is cold. The cold makes his leg more painful as if the shrapnel was still lodged in his thigh.

The best thing about the new office is it comes with living quarters, a two-bedroomed flat. George is grateful for that as it not only solves a problem of his, but he is sure Jessie thought it was a great idea seeing she was about to be kicked out of her boarding house. George appreciated the good fortune of the flat. It made him forget the pain in his leg for the time being.

He stared out of the window of his office. He could hear the hordes of people outside, talking and talking, their voices carried across the wind, their howls in the rain, their calls and cries, their daily lives. He could also hear the clatter of the overhead railway affectionately known as the Dockers' Umbrella. The smell of sea salt driven in by a westerly from the Mersey mixed with musty leather and aged mahogany. There were also the smells of fresh coffee from the Kardomah coffee shop owned by the Liverpool China and India Tea Company and hops from the nearby Higsons brewery. Oblivious to everything in the universe, rainwater splatters on the streets and fills the cracks of the cobblestones.

It's my city, he thinks, and George breathes in deeply, taking all the smells of the city into his lungs. The smell of the sea, of fish and salt, of pubs, of cigarette and pipe smoke, bad breath, of grease, of coal smoke, of the docks, of ships and the people that made their living from the sea, of molasses and whales, and not forgetting the local delicacy of rode haring. He could make out the acrid smell of factory smoke in the distance, and the stench of seagull and pigeon doo-doo.

His thoughts are interrupted on hearing ticking, a clockwork tick-tock, like a rhythmic pendulum clock. Looking up, he saw the grandfather clock generously donated by his good friend and companion Jessie Harper. *Hmmm, I'm not dreaming*, George thought. He knows Jessie is a highly educated woman and a renowned paranormal expert, specializing in the study of ghosts, poltergeists, and the supernatural. With their combined expertise, they are sure to make the agency a success. Or so he hopes.

PULLING ON THE CHAIN of his pocket watch and glancing at the watch face, George saw it was almost time to meet Jessie at the Kardomah. Grabbing his coat first, he wrapped himself in that before reaching up to the top of the coat stand to retrieve his black homburg hat. Then he retrieved his cane before locking the office door behind him and descending the steps into Dale Street.

JESSIE SPOTTED GEORGE at the front door of the Kardomah and waved to get his attention. He waved back before hanging his coat and hat. She had found a booth away from prying eyes and ears so they could speak freely about the new venture. She had already ordered two coffees so she was hoping George would soon bring her up to speed.

Once George had settled into the booth and put away his cane to his right so no one would knock it over, Jessie initiated the conversation. "George, I hope you know what you are doing. I mean these aren't the best of times to be opening a new business."

George sighed and after taking a deep breath, he talked incessantly. Clearly, he needed some moral support. "Granted, Jessie, I am throwing economic caution to the wind by opening a private detective agency in the city. But, you know, I always wanted to be a detective. Sadly, in 1919, the Liverpool City Police turned me down owing to my disability, my war wound. Now, I am forty-two years old, and determined to make the agency a success with your help. We have known each other a long time. You know my strengths. I was employed as a clerk in the Criminal Investigation Department at Liverpool's main police station in Hardman Street. Despite my limp and the cane that are permanent legacies of my war injury, I managed to get that job and over the years, I have got to know most of the criminals in the city. The thieves, burglars and fences."

"Excellent, but where do I come in to all this?"

"You are an intelligent woman, Jessie, with a good education and somewhat an expert on supernatural matters. In short, you would be an asset to the agency," George said.

"Right then but just two more things. My cat must be allowed to live with me at the flat, and two, you are now forty-two, George, and an eligible bachelor. You must have your admirers with those boyish good looks and impeccable good manners. I have my reputation to think of. I don't want anyone gossiping behind my back that we are shacked up together."

"Let me put your mind at rest, Jessie, I have no designs on you nor any other young woman."

"So, I'm ugly then?"

"No, of course not," George said looking at her auburn hair that fell to her shoulders. The conversation was interrupted by the waitress serving the two coffees.

GEORGE HAD KNOWN JESSIE for years and had always regarded her as a friend but now he looked at her across the table. He saw her in a new light and saw how attractive she was. Their parents had been friends and that's how Jessie and George happened to meet. He had thought of her as a sister that he never had... until now.

Jessie was at thirty-three, an attractive woman with auburn shoulder length hair. It was lightly permed as was the fashion of the day. She had a perfect figure for the day's fashions. She was tall and lean and wore her clothes with a defined upper waist that accentuated her small-medium size bust. She had no trace of an accent despite living in Liverpool all her life. She wasn't posh though. Jessie knew the vocabulary from A-Z of the 'Sailor Town' fishwives' bawdy lexicon. Sailor Town was an area of rows of dilapidated terraced houses set between Scotland Road and the docks. The area was renowned for drunkenness and fighting that usually happened once the sailor husband came home from the high seas. More accurately, a few weeks following the matelot's return. At first, all was fun and games especially if the sailor had brought an exotic souvenir home such as a monkey in a cage. The wife, kids, and neighbours were enthralled at the sight and antics of the monkey.

The days, then weeks dragged on with the sailor frequenting his usual drinking haunts. After a month or so, the sailor was drunk in the afternoon and the evenings. At that point. He, his wife, and his kids knew he would soon start to look for his next ticket: another voyage to the other side of the world. That was not only the sailor's life but also that of his family.

"The cat is welcome and so are you. I will have the locksmith put a lock on your bedroom door. That might help stop idle folks making up stories and gossiping," George said, leaving the money on the table as payment for the coffees. "Please excuse me. I have a meeting with Bill Roberts back at the office. Why don't you start packing your belongings at the boarding house?"

"Detective Sergeant Bill Roberts?" Jessie asked.

Chapter 3

BILL WAS ON TIME. GEORGE heard the knock on the office door and through the frosted glass, he could see the burly outline of Detective Sergeant Bill Roberts of the Liverpool City Police, so he called out, "Come in, Bill."

The Detective Sergeant entered the office taking in everything he could see just like the proficient detective he was. Bill seemed to fill up the room with his considerable presence. A presence even more enhanced by a heavy overcoat and Bill's favourite headgear, a pancake style flat cap. Bill always wore it and never tired of telling the tale of how it reminded him of his working-class roots in North Wales.

"Coffee, Bill?" George said.

"Only if you have a wee dram to spice it up," Bill said.

"Rum but no whiskey,"

"That'll do. I'm thankful for small mercies as I know you don't imbibe."

"Wait, I'll go and sort it out," George said, his back disappearing into the small kitchen. After the kettle stopped whistling, George came back holding a steaming cup that smelled something like coffee but not the exotic smell that emanates from the Kardomah. He went into the bottom drawer of his desk and retrieved a bottle of dark rum. Loosening the cap, he poured a decent measure into the coffee before handing it to Bill.

As Bill raised the cup to his lips, George said, "Careful. It's still hot."

"Only a cautious sip, George, until it cools down a bit." One careful and short sip later, Bill added, "This is so much better coffee than we had in the trenches, don't you think, George?"

"I guess so. I don't think about those days too much," George said.

"Look, George, we are great friends and always will be but I'm not going to put up with any nonsense from you, especially you."

"What do you mean?" George said, looking aghast.

"You do think about those days. I know you do. Don't get me wrong, you hide it well but at forty-two, you fear failure and being branded a worthless cripple. Don't get me wrong. You did a great job for us at CID Admin, but I knew you were so frustrated at being office-bound."

Bill Roberts is possibly the only person who could say this to George and get away with it. George had confided in only two people about his plans for the detective agency. Jessie, of course, and Detective Sergeant Bill Roberts. He had known Bill a long time too and they had soldiered together in WW1. George knew he owed his life to Bill Roberts. He and George served together in the 4th (Extra Reserve) Battalion, King's (Liverpool Regiment). It was Bill who rendered first aid and oversaw George's evacuation from the trenches at Ypres. For his actions that day, Bill received the Military Medal, an award for gallantry and devotion to duty when under fire in battle on land. He never talks about it. Not even to Jessie or George.

Bill Roberts was a thoughtful man and the same age as George. He looked even more thoughtful when smoking his pipe. Bill knew how frustrated George was sitting behind a desk all day and reading reports of how the detectives in the department had caught law breakers. So, when George asked for advice about the detective agency, Bill encouraged him.

"You should do it," Bill said, "in fact, I'll send the odd job your way when I can. You have got a head start on any competition because you know most of the criminals in the city through your work at Hardman Street. One favour though, just keep anything I tell you on the Q.T. I don't want to annoy the bosses."

"Of course, and that's good of you, Bill. That's encouraging at a time thousands are losing their jobs and I give up on mine voluntarily. By the way, I should also tell you I have asked Jessie to be my partner."

George saw Bill's jaw quiver momentarily. "Not that sort of partner, you idiot!"

Looking sheepish, Bill recovered quickly enough to say, "Maybe you ought to do that too. I mean you are an eligible bachelor."

"Don't be daft. Jessie's not interested," George said, "she is more interested in her study of the supernatural and that cat of hers."

"Maybe yes, maybe no," Bill said, "if you don't, I might, especially if she casts a spell on you."

"Bill, that's not funny. You can't go around saying she's a witch."

"I'm not. Keep your hair on, George. But that cat of hers does give me the heebie- jeebies."

Chapter 4

THE NEXT DAY GEORGE was in the office when he heard the footsteps. They were getting louder so up, not down towards the street. They weren't heavy either, so a woman. He wasn't expecting Jessie for another hour or so as she had to take her cat to the veterinary surgeon. The cat had the unusual name, for a cat, of Khan. Jessie did explain the origin of the cat's name. He was named after a hero in the Great War, a Khudadad Khan: the first Muslim soldier to receive the Victoria Cross when his small team of machine gunners stalled a German advance long enough to allow for British reinforcements to arrive in October 1914. George snapped out of his daydreaming to see a woman's outline through the frosted glass of the office door before he heard the bell tinkle. *At least that bell works*, he thought as he looked up at Jessie.

GESTURING TO GEORGE that she didn't need help to remove her coat, Jessie hung it on the coat stand close to the office door. "It's getting foggy out there, George," she said as she also placed her hat on the stand.

"Aye, I can almost taste it," George nodded. "Not good for business either."

"Be patient, George. You see it won't be long before you are busy on your first case."

"*Our* first case. I do hope so. Fancy a cuppa? I'll go and put the kettle on."

"I stand corrected. Yes, that would be nice," Jessie said.

Returning with a freshly brewed cup of tea, George said, "When do you think you will move into the flat?"

"We'll see. Let me think about it and I might have to ask Khan what he thinks."

"What? The cat talks?"

"George, dear. He's not any old black cat. He's rather special."

"You are always kidding me about your cat but if you like he can come and work here too."

"Tomorrow, George. My landlady is getting her knickers in a right twist about cats in general, so I'm packed. I'll be here bright and early."

THE NEXT DAY, GEORGE, Jessie, and Khan were in the office early. The fog had cleared leaving a light mist behind it. "What's Khan doing here?" George asked.

"George, what a short memory you have. Khan works here now." Noticing George's puzzled look, she added, "I told you, my landlady at the boarding house won't allow pets any longer. She claims they smell. She knows nothing about cats. It's humans and stray dogs that smell," Jessie harrumphed.

"I note you emphasised the word 'claims.' Is there another reason, Jessie?"

"My, you will make a great detective noticing little things like that. Promise me you won't make fun at what I'm about to say. I think Khan is my guide. Do you know what I am talking about?"

"No."

"It may seem a little strange, but Khan could be what is known as my familiar. A familiar spirit. He can see and sense things I am unable to see. So, he can guide me in things supernatural. In mediaeval times, I would have been called a witch and burned at the stake. But I'm not a witch. I am just blessed to have such a special cat."

"Thank you for the explanation. Thank goodness your landlady only wants you to leave and not making up stories about you and Khan. It's funny Bill was only just saying that Khan gives him the creeps."

"What about you, George, you don't think I am a witch, do you?"

"Far from it, and Khan is welcome." George knew it was pointless to argue with Jessie about cats especially Khan. "He's got a job then. I saw a rat on the stairs this morning when I opened the street door."

"His wages?" Jessie smiled.

"Milk and cat food, of course."

"You hear that, Khan?" You have a job and a new home." Khan purred loudly as if he understood. Perhaps he did.

The interview with Khan now over, they heard a loud bellowing voice, "Are you in, George? I don't want to waste any breath climbing these bloody stairs if you are out."

George and Jessie knew the voice belonged to Bill Roberts.

"We're in. Do you want a brew?" George shouted.

"Yes, the usual, three sugars and milk, cheers!"

"What? No rum?" George said.

"Not in tea. Only coffee."

"I'll do it," Jessie said, "it gives me a chance to give Khan a saucer of milk too as his welcome home treat."

Jessie served up fresh cups of tea and a plate of biscuits as all three settled down to talk, when George as curious as ever said, "What brings you here, Bill?"

"I nearly used the telephone, but I thought better to come and see you both in your new surroundings," Bill smiled. He continued, "After all, your office is only a few hundred yards away from mine. I have some news about a charity event, a garden party, and if you ask me, I think you should both attend. You never know who you will meet, and it may lead to some cases for you. It's not until next summer but you know how time flies so put it in your diary."

"Don't *misunderstand* because we are always grateful to see you in our office, aren't we, Jessie?" George said.

"Of course," Jessie nodded without knowing the rest of the story and heard George finish what he was saying, "but you could have told us that over the phone." Now the *misunderstand* bit fell into place.

Bill continued, "The inspector at Hatton Garden doesn't want to send any police officers as he thinks gatherings like that are a waste of time. But mark my words. All the city's bigwigs will be there. It's a good opportunity for you two to hand out plenty of business cards.

"The other thing is I managed to persuade the inspector to give you a weekly missing persons list. That is where you can earn money when you track them down. It will keep you going and help pay the rent."

"Well, thank you, Bill," Jessie said.

"Have you got a name and address for this gathering of the high and mighty?" George said.

"Not on me. It's some rectory in the Old Swan area so not far. I'll tell you what... I'll call you later with the details and the vicar who is hosting this do," Bill said.

IT WAS FOUR IN THE afternoon when Bill called. Jessie answered, "Dale Street Private Investigations."

"Sounds fancy," Bill said. It took a moment for the meaning of 'fancy' to sink in, then Bill added, "Here is the information I promised you. The priest is called Reverend Albert Bennett. He's the vicar of Liverpool's St. Mary's Church The vicarage phone number is Old Swan 512." Jessie wrote it all down on a pad of writing paper kept next to the telephone. "Thanks, Bill. I will get in touch with him nearer the time of the garden party."

Chapter 5

JOYCE AND ELLEN STOOD in the foggy streets of Liverpool, their coats and cloche hats providing a faint sense of comfort against the chill of the night air. The buildings around them seemed to disappear into the fog, as if the city that had been so alive during the day had been swallowed up by a great grey beast.

Ellen slipped her hand into Joyce's, her grip warm and comforting. They stood in the stillness of the fog-filled night, listening to the not-too-distant sounds of a ship's horn and the cries of seagulls.

They both knew why they were here. They had come seeking something, a piece of the puzzle that would bring them closer to understanding the truth. A truth about their mother.

A light suddenly burned through the fog, and they saw the silhouette of a man emerging from the shadows. He was dressed in an old-fashioned suit, a bowler hat perched atop his bald head. He beckoned them over with a curt nod of his head and they both walked towards him, their feet crunching the cobblestones beneath their feet.

The man studied them carefully, his cold eyes taking in the details of their attire and the expressions on their faces. Finally, he nodded and reached into his pocket, pulling out a crumpled envelope. "You've been summoned," he said gruffly, handing the envelope to Ellen.

Inside was a single yellowed piece of paper, a page seemingly torn from a book, carefully folded yet still indicating a hint of jagged edge. Ellen handed the paper to Joyce and the man nodded, motioning for them to follow him. "Where are you taking us?" Ellen said.

"All your questions will be answered when we get there," the mystery man said. He led them through the fog, their journey in search of the truth finally beginning.

All the man was prepared to add was he was an emissary sent by a one member of a secret society that had a vested interest in keeping its affairs under wraps. He added that the member has a conscience and had no desire to see the daughters of Rosie O'Grady orphaned unnecessarily.

The trio emerged from the fog onto a deserted street that seemed to belong to a Dickensian era. The buildings were tall and foreboding with blackened windows and heavy gates. The man led them to a building at the end of the street, where they climbed a flight of stairs and entered a dimly lit room filled with smoke and the sound of murmured voices.

Ellen and Joyce felt out of place in their prim dresses, surrounded by men in expensive suits and polished shoes. The man who had led them there disappeared into the back of the room, leaving them alone to fend for themselves. They took some empty nearby seats, huddling together for warmth.

As they sat, they heard snippets of conversation from those around them. "The gossip about the stolen painting must stop," said one voice. "We can't afford any setbacks," said another, and yet another said, "... aye, even if we have to make them disappear for good."

A chill ran down Ellen's spine as she listened to their callous disregard for human life. She knew then that they had stumbled upon something bigger than they had imagined, that her mother seemed to have a secret life, if not living a double life, and was possibly involved in something dark.

Chapter 6

TIME HAD FLOWN JUST like the sage detective, Bill Roberts, had predicted. It was now July and Liverpool was enjoying a heatwave. The heat of the day faded as the sun dipped below the horizon, its golden rays caressing the vibrant petals of roses and lilies as Jessie made her way along the winding path. The pleasant aroma of freshly baked scones wafted through the air, mingling with laughter and cheerful voices in the vicarage garden. It was a large garden, two gardens, really, if you count the inner walled garden as a second garden. The garden, or gardens whichever you prefer, looked splendid now that the ornamental lamps were switched on as the dusk rapidly approached.

Jessie smiled, nodding in greeting at familiar faces. It had been too long since her last social event, and she relished the opportunity to reconnect with friends from her librarian days and even former neighbours. Even Khan, her incorrigible feline companion, had deemed the occasion important enough to accompany her, prowling about the garden with his usual air of mystery.

"Jessie, dear, you look lovely this evening!" Clara Bennett, the vicar's wife, emerged from the crowd, clasping Jessie's hands warmly in her own. "I'm so glad you could make it."

"Thank you, Clara. I wouldn't have missed it." Jessie returned the smile, noticing the faint lines of worry etched into her friend's brow. "Is everything all right? You seem rather preoccupied."

Clara waved a hand dismissively. "Oh, it's nothing. Just the usual parish affairs keeping me busy."

"If there's anything I can do to help, please don't hesitate to ask."

"How kind of you." Clara's eyes softened. "But there's no need to worry yourself. Tonight is meant for enjoyment and merriment!"

A loud shriek pierced the air before Jessie could respond. Gasps and cries of alarm rippled through the crowd as guests stared towards the walled garden entrance, hands flying to cover gaping mouths.

Jessie's heart lurched. She gripped Clara's arm, exchanging a look of dread, and they rushed forward with the rest of the guests. Time seemed to slow as Jessie pushed through, her pulse pounding in her ears.

Finally, she broke through to the front, barely registering the chaos around her. There, lying motionless on the ground, was a woman —a knife protruding from her chest, but strangely there was no blood to be seen anywhere.

"Poor Rosie," Clara Bennett said. "She was such a hard worker who had endured more hardship than anyone deserved, only to meet such a tragic end."

Panic rose in Jessie's throat as she stared at the lifeless body but uttered, "You knew her?"

"Yes, Rosie O'Grady. She was a parishioner here and worked in the vicarage. In fact, she was such a good worker we allowed her to live in. She had her own room."

A firm hand clasped Jessie's shoulder, jolting her from the nightmare unfolding before her eyes. She looked up to find George's concerned gaze, laced with determination.

"We have a murder to solve," is all George said.

Jessie blinked, Rosie's face fading into the concerned visages of guests surrounding them. She took a steadying breath and steeled her nerves.

George was right. Rosie deserved justice, and Jessie would not rest until the culprit was brought to justice. She only prayed the hunt would not prove too harrowing, with supernatural forces already gathering in the shadows. The nightmare was only just beginning.

Jessie surveyed the scene, taking in every detail. The knife was an ornate silver affair, buried up to the hilt in Rosie's chest. No signs of a struggle, aside from the trampled grass where guests had rushed to the body.

"Did anyone see what happened?" she asked. The guests glanced at each other nervously. Finally, a stout woman in a feathered hat spoke up. "It was awful sudden, it was. One minute Rosie was chatting away, next she let out this terrible shriek and collapsed."

"I saw something move in the bushes, just before," a timid voice piped up. Jessie turned to find the vicarage gardener, wringing his cap in calloused hands. "Thought it might've been a cat, but then..." He trailed off, eyes wide.

"Did you see anyone emerge from the bushes or the walled garden?" George asked. The gardener shook his head. "But I heard something, rustling about. Then a shape moved past, too fast to see proper."

Jessie and George exchanged a glance. The gardener was not one to imagine things. If he said he saw movement, they could trust there had been something there.

"Thank you," Jessie said. "Please don't speak to anyone else about this. We don't want speculation running rampant. We will undoubtedly wish to speak to you again at some point."

The guests began to disperse at the urging of Reverend Bennett, who approached with a grave expression. "Dreadful business," he said, sighing. "Will you look into this, as I hear you, Jessie, are somewhat an expert on the paranormal?"

Jessie nodded. "We will get to the bottom of this. You have my word. But we will need the blessing of Detective Sergeant Roberts to take charge of the case."

As uniformed constables began examining the scene, Jessie took George's arm, leaning close to whisper. "There are supernatural forces at work here. This woman was killed too swiftly, too neatly, for any human hand. How many knife wounds have you seen with no blood?

There are other signs too, but I will talk to you later about that." Her eyes hardened. "We're hunting a killer with powers beyond our understanding. And we must stop them before they strike again."

THE NEXT MORNING, JESSIE sat at her desk in the office with a cup of strong tea, reviewing the details of the case. George had left early to interview some of Rosie's acquaintances, hoping to turn up clues as to why she might have been targeted.

Jessie rubbed her temples, frustration mounting. The supernatural angle complicated matters. There were no convenient footprints or other clues to examine, no logical sequence of events to deduce. She was operating in the dark, groping for answers that seemed perpetually out of reach.

With a sigh, she stood and straightened her skirt, setting her jaw in determination. She would get nowhere moping about. It was time to have another look at the crime scene.

THE VICARAGE GARDEN seemed eerie in daylight, roses and lilies drooping where they had been trampled the night before. Jessie walked slowly around the perimeter, watching and listening for any disturbances in the ether, and hence any supernatural clues.

There. A strange chill, and for just a moment, the air seemed to shimmer. She whipped around, but it had already vanished. Frowning, Jessie knelt to examine the ground. There, almost hidden in the grass, was a long, black feather. Her eyes widened as she plucked it from the ground, turning it over in her hands. Her studies told her, only one creature had feathers like these. A creature rarely seen but often felt, whose presence was heralded by a deathly cold: An angel of death.

Jessie's heart raced as she pocketed the feather. An angel of death at the vicarage garden party. This was worse than she had feared.

She made her way over to where the body had lain, now marked by a rust-coloured stain on the grass. A stain from what, she did not know. Kneeling again, she closed her eyes and took a deep breath, trying to detect any lingering traces of paranormal energy.

There. A strange, unpleasant tingle at the base of her skull. She latched onto it, following it through the ether like a bloodhound on the scent. It led away from the garden, out into the street, before fading into nothingness.

Jessie opened her eyes with a start. Blast. She had lost the trail. But at least now she knew the killer had fled the scene. This was no mere haunting. They were dealing with a living, breathing entity, one with sinister intentions and formidable powers.

She stood and dusted off her skirt, glancing over at the vicarage. Reverend Bennett was watching her from an upstairs window, his brow furrowed with concern. When he noticed her looking, he gave a brief nod and withdrew.

Jessie sighed. The vicar knew more than he was letting on, she was sure of it. But getting information out of him would be like pulling teeth. Perhaps George would have better luck.

Speaking of George, where had he gotten to? He was supposed to be here by now. She scanned the garden but could not spot his familiar tweed suit. With rising alarm, she set off in search of her partner, hoping against hope that he hadn't gotten into trouble. This was turning out to be a far more dangerous affair than either of them had bargained for.

Jessie quickened her pace as she combed through the vicarage garden. Yesterday's scream was still fresh in her mind, ringing in her ears like a banshee's wail. She had to find George before it was too late. Late for what exactly, she didn't know but deep down she was fearful.

There! A glimpse of tweed disappearing behind a hedge. She raced over and peered through the foliage, relief flooding over her as she spotted George crouched down, scrutinizing the ground.

"George, thank heavens I found you."

He glanced up, peering at her over the rim of his spectacles. "Ah, Jessie. Come have a look at this."

She ducked under the hedge and joined him, noticing several long, crimson scratches marring the otherwise pristine lawn. "Claw marks," she breathed.

George nodded. "And more than that. There are traces of sulphur in the air, and the temperature has dropped significantly in this area."

"A manifestation of some kind, then." Her heart quickened as the pieces fell into place. They were not merely dealing with an ordinary killer. "It seems our murderer has paranormal abilities."

"Or is working with someone who does." George stood, brushing dirt from his trousers. "I fear this will be a far more dangerous case than we had anticipated."

Jessie bit her lip, staring at the claw marks. What had they gotten themselves into? She steeled herself, squaring her shoulders. No matter the risk, they had a duty to bring Rosie O'Grady's killer to justice.

"We must inform Bill Roberts about this new development," she said. "He will need to take extra precautions if there are supernatural forces at work."

George nodded. "Quite right. We should also have a chat with the vicar and see what else he might be keeping from us."

Jessie frowned. This was turning out to be a most peculiar case indeed.

THE REVEREND BENNETT invited Jessie and George to partake in tea and biscuits outside on the vicarage patio.

"How could this happen? "Poor Rosie, it must have been the work of a madman," Reverend Bennett said. He hesitated but then said, "I have heard rumours she was connected to a secret society."

"Rumours?" Jessie said with an unmistakeable look of disdain on her face. She bit back a sigh, knowing the truth was far more complicated than that. She saw Reverend Bennett was looking pale and shaken, clutching at his silver cross. His eyes seemed to light up at the mere fact he was talking to Jessie and George.

Grasping Jessie's arm, he said in hushed tones, "You must help us! This is clearly the work of dark forces."

We know," Jessie said gently, prying his fingers from her arm. "There are signs of paranormal involvement here. Did you see or hear anything unusual before the murder?"

The vicar shook his head, distress etched into his features. "No, nothing until that terrible scream. But you mention the claw marks, the drop in temperature—it can only be the work of evil." His eyes pleaded with them. "You must find the fiend responsible for this at once!"

"We will do our best," George assured him. "For now, please provide us with a complete guest list including those invited but failed to attend. We need to speak with anyone who might have information about what occurred."

Reverend Bennett nodded, still pale but seeming to gain control of himself. "Yes, yes, of course. Please let me know if there's anything else I can do to help. This is a dark day for our village. I still call Old Swan a village for that is what it was at one time." He sighed, gazing sorrowfully into the distance. "She was a pillar of the church. We shall all miss her greatly."

"Our condolences," Jessie said. "We will get to the bottom of this, I promise you."

The vicar's lips pressed into a thin line as he nodded. "I shall pray you succeed."

Jessie suppressed a grimace, hoping they would need more than prayers to prevail against an enemy with paranormal powers. This was turning out to be an altogether more dangerous affair than she had bargained for.

JESSIE AND GEORGE MOVED away from Reverend Bennett towards a secluded corner of the garden. "This has gone too far," Jessie said in a low voice. "Black magic, demons—we're out of our depth. Not to mention secret societies, we should leave this to the police."

"And let the killer escape?" George shook his head. "We can't do that. Not when there's a chance we could stop them."

Jessie bit her lip, torn between her desire to see justice done and her instincts for self-preservation. Before she could reply, a gruff voice interrupted them.

"I couldn't help overhearing your conversation." Detective Sergeant Bill Roberts emerged from the shadows of the towering poplar trees, a grim expression on his face. "And I'm afraid I must agree with George. This is bigger than any ordinary murder. You two seem to have a knack for dealing with the, shall we say, peculiar. I think we need your help on this one."

Despite her misgivings, Jessie felt a surge of pride at the detective's praise. If they could solve this case, it would be a triumph for their fledgling agency. She glanced at George and saw her own determination reflected in his eyes. They were in this together, for better or for worse.

"Very well," Jessie said, turning back to Detective Roberts. "Where would you like us to start?"

The detective nodded, relief flickering across his craggy features. "Take another look at the crime scene. Look for anything out of the ordinary. Hell, what am I saying? You know what-is-what far better than I do. I'll organize interviews with the guests and staff in the meantime." He paused, meeting Jessie's gaze. "Be careful. I suspect we're dealing with dark forces here." With that ominous warning, Roberts strode off.

"We can't take another look at the body in situ because poor Rosie is now in the mortuary, but let's think, George, what did we see?"

"She was on her back, arms splayed, the hilt of a knife protruding from her chest. Her eyes were open, gazing sightlessly up at the dusky sky. There's was no blood. The knife wound should have caused significant bleeding, but her dress was pristine," George recited as if looking at an indelible vision stamped upon his memory cells.

"Impossible," she breathed. "No mortal wound could remain bloodless. This was evidence of paranormal forces at work. Let's go and speak again with the gardener. He may have remembered something helpful."

They found the gardener, Thomas, clutching a cup of tea in the kitchen. He was a stout, middle-aged man with kind eyes and a ruddy complexion, but now he still seemed shaken. As Jessie and George questioned him, he twisted his cap in his hands, words tumbling out in a rush.

"The outside lighting was on so I thought I would check on the roses, see, when I heard these odd noises coming from the azalea bushes. Rustling and scratching. I went to investigate, and the bushes started shaking like mad, but there weren't no animals or person there. Then I heard this unearthly shriek and ran toward the sound. And there was poor Rosie, stabbed and dead without a drop of blood, God rest her soul. It were like she were attacked by an invisible beast!" Thomas crossed himself, trembling.

"Did you see any shadows or spectral figures?" Jessie asked gently.

Thomas shook his head. "Nothing of the sort, miss. But I tell you, it were the work of dark forces. No ordinary evil could do such a thing."

His tale sent a chill down Jessie's spine. An invisible, malevolent presence and a bloodless corpse. This was shaping up to be one of the most frightening and perplexing cases.

Jessie pondered the gardener's account as they made their way back to the vicarage garden. "An invisible attacker and a bloodless body suggest supernatural elements at work," she said. "Yet the noises

Thomas described were quite physical. Whatever entity was involved likely has the ability to manifest physically at times, then vanish at will."

"You think we're dealing with a spirit that can turn corporeal?" George asked with a frown. "That does sound rather far-fetched."

"I know it's strange, but people have encountered such phenomena before. And there are clues that point to a paranormal motive." On entering the walled garden, Jessie's gaze settled on a symbol etched into the dirt near the azalea bushes. An inverted pentagram inside a circle—often used in occult rituals. Her eyes widened as she spotted another symbol and another, creating a trail that led back towards the vicarage.

"Look, George. Satanic symbols. Could it be Rosie O'Grady delved into dark magic? Perhaps she invoked malicious forces that turned against her?"

George stared at the symbols, shaking his head. "I don't know, Jessie. This all seems rather—"

"Far-fetched? Impossible?" Jessie sighed. "I understand your scepticism. But we can't ignore the signs. We must investigate the secret society Rosie was involved with. That's where we'll find answers." She took his hand, giving it a squeeze. "You'll see. There are more things in heaven and earth than are dreamt of in your philosophy."

George gazed into Jessie's determined eyes and managed a wry smile. "Touché. Very well, my dear Prince Hamlet. Let's see where this trail of occult clues leads us. Or perhaps I should throw in a 'perchance' in addition?"

Jessie grinned, buoyed by George's willingness to set aside his doubts. With his level head and her book knowledge of all things strange and sinister, they would get to the bottom of this murder yet. The game was afoot!

Jessie and George followed the trail of occult symbols through the vicarage garden and into the churchyard, where the signs seemed to disappear. They searched the area thoroughly but found no trace of anything unusual.

"Blast!" Jessie stomped her foot in frustration. "The trail has gone cold."

"Not necessarily," George said. "We know the symbols led us to the churchyard. Perhaps we should investigate inside the church. Rosie O'Grady was a devoted parishioner, after all."

"Brilliant deduction!" Jessie grasped George's hand and squeezed it. "You're getting quite good at this sleuthing business."

George blushed at the praise as they entered the hallowed ground of St. Mary's Church. Everything appeared normal at first glance—pews aligned in neat rows, and the altar bare and unadorned.

Then Jessie noticed something odd about the floor tiles. "Look, the tiles in front of the altar form a five-pointed star. And there—a candlestick holder askew from its usual position. I'll wager the secret society held their occult rituals right here!"

George peered at the suspicious details, furrowing his brow. "You could be right. But how do we find out more about this secret society and their connection to Rosie O'Grady?"

"We dig deeper," Jessie said with determination. "There are always clues, if one knows where to look. And I have a feeling the answers lie close at hand, hidden in plain sight. We must uncover them before the killer strikes again!"

Jessie smiled, relishing the thrill of the hunt. Together, she and George would solve this murder, come hell or high water. The game was still afoot, and she wouldn't rest until they emerged victorious.

Chapter 7

JESSIE AND GEORGE VISITED the vicarage again the next day intending to interview all the staff in the employ of the Reverend Bennett. First, they strolled around the garden to clear their heads ready for a bout of interrogating the staff. The gardener, Thomas, saw them first and waved a hearty cheerio, he then walked away but suddenly stopped and walked back to them.

"Thomas, are you all right?" Jessie said.

"Not really, miss..." Thomas stuttered, "please don't tell anyone bur I found this clutched in Rosie's hand." He handed over a gold-coloured trinket on a chain.

Jessie examined the jewellery and noted the familiar symbol etched into its surface. It was the same peculiar marking she'd previously found near the garden. She could feel her heart pounding as she realized Rosie had gotten too close to a secret someone wanted kept, and now she was dead, a victim silenced by the sinister forces lurking within this village's pristine facade.

Jessie sighed, shaking off the chill that crept down her spine. There would be time enough for morbid reflection later—right now, they had a murder to solve.

Patiently waiting for the right moment, she turned to Detective Sergeant Bill Roberts, who was quietly questioning one of the maids hovering in the doorway. "Did anyone have it in for Rosie?" Jessie asked.

Bill glanced over; brow furrowed. "Hard to say. Rosie had her share of enemies, but according to the staff, she'd been on her best behaviour recently." His gaze softened, "Seems she was trying to turn things around, find honest work. Shame it had to end this way."

"Yes, well, we'll make sure her killer faces justice." Jessie looked around the room again, searching for anything the killer or Rosie might have left behind. After all, Jessie thought, Rosie did work here and as for the killer, he or she may have worked here too. There, near the fireplace—a scrap of paper, tucked half under the edge of the rug.

Heart pounding, she retrieved a pair of gloves from her handbag and picked it up, angling it to catch the light. A few words were scrawled across the page in a hasty hand:

The circle meets at moonrise. Tell no one.

Her eyes widened. A clue, perhaps, to the identity of Rosie's secret society and a chance to infiltrate their sinister ranks.

"Find something interesting?" Bill asked, coming up beside her.

"Possibly." Jessie passed him the note, watching as his eyes narrowed. "Seems there's more to this village than meets the eye. And Rosie was caught right in the middle of it."

"Looks that way." Bill sighed, "Reckon this is shaping up to be a rough one. You sure you're up for it?"

Jessie lifted her chin, gaze hardening with determination. "I have to be. For Rosie's sake, and whoever else these monsters may target if we don't stop them."

No matter the cost, she would get to the truth. The circle would soon find they had made a grave mistake in underestimating her resolve.

The game was on.

Having had one breakthrough in the search, Jessie took a steadying breath and looked around the room with a keen eye, searching for anything the police might have missed.

"Let's start with the basics," she said. "Look for anything out of place. Secret compartments, hidden doors, clues that might point us to who Rosie really was."

Bill nodded and moved to examine the bookshelf, running his fingers along the spines of the dusty tomes. Jessie crouched by the desk, sorting through the scattered papers for anything noteworthy. Most were receipts, bills, the mundane scraps of life. But tucked between the pages of an old ledger, she found a photograph.

It showed Rosie and two other women in front of the vicarage, arms linked and smiles bright. A startling resemblance in their features suggested they were sisters. On the back, Rosie had scrawled a date from over twenty years ago.

"Bill, come look at this." She passed him the photo, a chill running down her spine. "Rosie had two sisters. And from the looks of it, they haven't been here in a long time."

His eyes widened as the implications sank in. "You don't think—"

"It's possible." Jessie rose, dusting off her trousers. "We need to know more about Rosie's family. Two sisters who vanished from the village without a trace? I doubt that's a coincidence."

"Agreed." Bill handed back the photo, a frown marring his brow. "This case just got a lot more complicated."

Jessie tucked the photo into her pocket, determination settling into her bones. The secrets surrounding Rosie's death ran deep, tangled up with the mysteries of her hidden past. But she would find the truth, no matter how painful it proved to be.

For Rosie, and for the two sisters who had long ago disappeared without a trace. The game was on.

Chapter 8

REVEREND BENNETT USHERED them into his study, offering tea and biscuits with a trembling hand. His face was pale and drawn, aged beyond his years. Guilt and grief warred in his eyes as he regarded them over the rim of his teacup.

"Please accept my condolences," Jessie said gently. "I know how close you and Rosie were."

The vicar flinched, nearly dropping his cup. "Yes, quite. A terrible loss." He took a long sip of tea before continuing. "As I told the police, Rosie volunteered to help organize the garden party. She was acting strangely in the days leading up to it, secretive and distracted."

"Strangely how?" Bill asked.

"She kept slipping away to make telephone calls and receive mysterious visitors." The vicar worried his lower lip. "I didn't think much of it at the time. Rosie always had her little secrets. But now..."

"You believe her unusual behaviour may have been connected to her death," Jessie finished. The vicar nodded; misery etched into the lines of his face.

"If I'd paid closer attention, perhaps I could have prevented this tragedy."

"Don't blame yourself," Bill said gruffly. "You couldn't have known."

"Thank you for your kindness." The vicar sighed. "I wish I could offer more information, but I'm afraid that's all I know."

Jessie set down her teacup, thinking fast. "Might we speak with your staff then? They may have insights we lack."

"Of course, anything to help." The vicar rose on creaking knees. "I'll take you to them straightaway."

They followed him downstairs to the kitchens, where two women were busy scrubbing pots and pans. At the sight of the vicar, they dropped into curtsies, murmuring, "Reverend Bennett."

"Please speak freely with Miss Harper and Mr Jenkins about the night of the garden party," the vicar said. "They're investigating Rosie's death and need your help."

The older woman, Mrs Smith, frowned. "It's not our place to gossip about such things."

"Nonsense. These people want to find Rosie's killer same as us." The vicar gave her a stern look. "Now tell them what they need to know."

Mrs Smith sniffed but relented. "Very well. What do you want to know?"

Jessie smiled, grateful for the vicar's aid. The staff were sure to know details about the tensions between Rosie and the guests. This was the break they needed. The game was still on.

Jessie's keen eyes scanned the kitchen. "Did anything seem amiss the night of the party? Were there any arguments or disagreements?"

"Oh yes," the younger maid, Sally, piped up. "Mrs Bartlett and Rosie had words about the floral arrangements. Rosie wanted lilies, but Mrs Bartlett insisted on roses. Nearly came to blows, they did."

"And the alderman, Mr Campbell, complained about the menu for the grand dinner in August," Mrs Smith added. "Wanted pheasant instead of duck. Rosie wouldn't hear of it. Told him if he didn't like it, he could dine elsewhere. Not that it was any of her business, but she did seem too familiar with Mr Campbell and other local bigwigs."

Jessie frowned. Multiple tensions and unresolved conflicts. This case was growing more complex.

"Did Rosie seem worried or upset afterwards?" George asked.

"She did," Sally said. "Stomped out to the garden, she did, muttering under her breath. When I took tea outside later, I noticed peculiar symbols drawn in the dirt near where she was killed."

"Symbols?" Jessie's heart quickened. "What did they look like?"

Sally shrugged. "Odd shapes and such. Lines and circles connected together."

"Can you show us?" Jessie could barely contain her excitement. Another clue!

"Of course, follow me." Sally led them outside to a patch of disturbed earth close to the walled garden.

There, etched into the soil, were several alchemical symbols, including a triangle within a circle. Jessie gasped, recognizing them at once.

"These are occult symbols used in supernatural rituals." Her eyes gleamed with determination. The paranormal twist in this mystery deepened. The game was definitely afoot.

Jessie's mind raced as she examined the peculiar symbols. What did they signify? A ritual? A curse? She needed answers.

"Did Rosie have any interest in the occult?" she asked Sally.

The young maid shook her head. "Not that I'm aware of. She was a good Christian woman."

"There must be something we're missing." Jessie gazed at the symbols, a piece of the puzzle still eluding her.

"Let's search her room again," George suggested. "Look for anything unusual that could point to her involvement in secret societies or dark magic."

"An excellent idea." Jessie hurried inside, George on her heels.

They combed through Rosie's belongings, checking inside books, under furniture, behind paintings. Jessie's keen eyes settled on the jewellery box, recalling it had seemed lighter than its contents suggested. She ran her fingers along its edges and seams, searching for hidden compartments.

"Aha!" Her index finger snagged on a mechanism, and a concealed drawer slid open. Inside was a faded photograph of three young girls and a woman who could only be their mother. Rosie.

"Joyce and Ellen," Jessie breathed, blinking back tears. After all these years, she had found them at last.

George peered at the photo. "You know these girls?"

"They're my sisters. I haven't seen them since I was a child." Jessie clutched the photo to her chest, overjoyed and heartsick all at once. "We were separated when our parents died or so I was told by my adopted parents. I never dreamed I'd find them here, or that Rosie was our mother."

"Your mother?" George's eyes widened. "But how is that possible? Why didn't she tell you?"

"I don't know." Jessie shook her head, emotions tumbling through her. "None of this makes sense. But I intend to find out the truth." Her gaze landed on a folded paper tucked beneath the photo. She opened it with trembling fingers.

The message was short but startling:

Dig beneath the old oak at midnight.

A secret meeting. A buried treasure. Occult symbols. And now a cryptic note pointing to her own family. This was no ordinary murder mystery. Dark secrets lurked beneath the surface, and Jessie feared she was in over her head. The game had turned dangerous, but she couldn't stop now. She had to know the truth.

Chapter 9

DETECTIVE SERGEANT Bill Roberts had gathered most of the garden party guests in the billiards room of the vicarage and instructed them to wait whilst he, Jessie, and George conducted the search of the vicarage and Rosie's room. The guests were unaware of Khan's presence.

Khan prowled among the guests. His paws silent on the floorboards as he listened in on hushed conversations. Most discussed the murder in shocked and hushed tones, but a few hinted at deeper tensions.

Khan found Lady Cavendish and Reverend Bennett engaged in a heated debate. "You had no right to involve her in this," Lady Cavendish hissed. "She was going to expose everything."

The vicar gripped his Bible until his knuckles turned white. "Rosie knew the risks. She chose her own path."

"And now she's paid the price for your foolish ambitions," Lady Cavendish shot back. "This has gone too far, and I won't be a part of it any longer." With that, she swept from the room in a flurry of silk and indignation.

Khan's ears pricked up. Rosie was involved with their secret ambitions, whatever those might be, and had threatened to expose the truth. It seemed Lady Cavendish had wanted out, while the vicar pushed forward relentlessly. Motives for murder, indeed. Khan decided he had heard enough so wandered outside in his cloak of invisibility.

IN THE GARDEN, KHAN found Colonel Windsor and Mr. Bartholomew engaged in a similarly tense exchange. "She didn't have the right to blackmail us," Colonel Windsor growled. "Threatening to reveal secrets that could ruin us all."

"We're in this together," Bartholomew hissed. "If she talked, we'd all hang." The Colonel fell silent, and they parted ways with wary glances.

Blackmail. Threats of exposure. Secrets that could ruin lives and send people to the gallows. Rosie had dangerous knowledge, and now she had paid the ultimate price for it. Khan had uncovered a nest of motives, and this mystery ran far deeper than any of them had imagined.

KHAN PADDED INTO THE room, his bright green eyes glancing between Jessie and George. "I have news," he meowed. "Lady Cavendish and Colonel Windsor were arguing in the gardens. It seems the colonel discovered Rosie's blackmail scheme and threatened to expose the group's activities to protect his reputation."

"So, the colonel had motive and means," Jessie said. "Perhaps he killed Rosie to keep her silent."

"There's more," Khan continued. "Mr. Bartholomew was later seen carrying a heavy sack toward the old oak grove. Its contents seemed to struggle and cry out."

Jessie gasped. "The body! Bartholomew must have moved Rosie's corpse to set the stage for her dramatic discovery."

"This proves they were all involved," George said, "but we still don't know who dealt the fatal blow."

"The vicar is suspiciously absent from these reports," Jessie observed. "His role in this conspiracy remains unclear. We must question him again."

Khan purred in agreement. "I will keep watch on our suspects and listen for any further revelations." With a flick of his tail, the cat vanished from view.

"Khan's intelligence may prove invaluable," George said. "But we must be careful. Desperate killers may target anyone who gets too close to the truth."

"It's an ingenious plan for her body to be moved to create a spectacle at the party the next day. A perfect scene of chaos to cover up the true motive and throw suspicion off the guilty parties. So, yes, they are dangerous and desperate killers," Jessie said.

George nodded. "An ingenious plan. But they made mistakes, and Rosie left behind clues that led us to the truth."

"Yes, important clues. Do you think we should continue to search for more in Rosie's room?" Jessie said.

Chapter 10

JESSIE AND GEORGE CREPT once more into Rosie's dimly lit room, searching for clues. Their eyes scoured the room, landing on a stack of old books, the same jewellery box, and a framed photograph on Rosie's bedside table.

Jessie picked up the photo, brushing away the dust. It showed Rosie and several stern-faced strangers dressed in black robes, standing before a crumbling stone altar.

"The secret society," Jessie breathed. "These must be its members."

George peered over her shoulder, scrutinizing each figure. "Note the insignia on their robes. That symbol matches the ones found near the garden."

"And look," Jessie said, "isn't that Mr. Bartholomew on the far left? The vicar lied about his involvement."

"He won't be the only one." George took the photo and compared it to the guest list. "Here we have a botanist, a professor, a wealthy widow, even a member of Parliament. All posing as upstanding citizens while engaging in these depraved rituals."

Jessie's eyes flashed. "For too long, the powerful have exploited the weak, keeping their misdeeds hidden behind closed doors. But their era of secrecy ends tonight."

"We have enough evidence to expose them," George said, "but we must take care. Desperate villains like these will stop at nothing to protect themselves."

"Then we shall have to stop at nothing to bring them to justice." Jessie's hands curled into fists, rage and determination mingling in her veins. "For Rosie, and for all their victims, we will tear down the walls of their depraved sanctuary once and for all."

WHILE JESSIE AND GEORGE examined the photo, Khan prowled through the vicarage. His paws made no sound on the wooden floorboards as he slipped into the vicar's study and wound between the shelves.

There, behind a heavy oak cabinet, he spotted a narrow opening in the wall. His whiskers twitched. A hidden passageway.

Khan let out a pleased meow. His hunch had been correct. He slid into the passage and padded down a winding stone staircase into the bowels of the building.

At the bottom, the staircase opened into a vast underground chamber. Candles flickered across dusty tomes and peculiar artifacts that hissed with dark energy. A pentagram had been etched into the floor, still stained with the blood of past rituals.

Khan narrowed his eyes. Powerful magic had been performed here; the kind that left echoes of suffering behind. His fur stood on end as he crept forward, detecting the presence of spirits trapped against their will.

A low, sinister laugh echoed through the chamber. "Well, well. What have we here?"

Khan whipped around to find a translucent figure in a tattered robe leering at him. The spirit's eyes glowed a venomous red, and a twisted grin stretched across its skeletal face.

"A curious cat," it rasped, "meddling in affairs that do not concern you. Be warned, furry one, lest you end up like the others who dared to disrupt our work."

The spirit lunged straight at Khan, spectral hands outstretched and crackling with malevolent energy. Khan yowled and darted away just in time, scrambling up the staircase with the spirit in hot pursuit.

He burst into Rosie's room, fur on end, as Jessie and George looked up in alarm. But when they saw nothing behind Khan, they exchanged a puzzled glance.

"What's gotten into him?" Jessie asked. Khan meowed urgently, trying to warn them of the danger that lurked below. But to no avail. His words could not reach human ears. His powers had failed.

The spirit's laughter echoed up from the hidden chamber, a grim promise of retribution. Khan shuddered. They would soon regret disturbing this secret society and the sinister forces it commanded.

Jessie frowned as Khan bolted out of the room and down the hall. "Something's spooked him. We should check the vicarage again before leaving."

George nodded. "There may be clues we've overlooked. And if there are spirits about, as the vicar believes, Khan likely sensed their presence."

They made their way downstairs, where Khan sat before the doorway to the hidden chamber, hackles raised. He meowed loudly and swatted at the air, but Jessie and George could detect nothing amiss.

"Easy now, Khan." Jessie reached down to pet him, but he hissed and swatted at her hand, eyes fixed on the entrance to the chamber.

Puzzled, Jessie and George entered the room. As before, it was empty save for the ancient tomes and strange relics lining the shelves. But a strange chill had settled over the space, and the hairs on the back of Jessie's neck prickled.

A floorboard creaked behind them. They whipped around to find a dark figure looming in the doorway, shrouded entirely in black. No face peered out from beneath the hood.

Jessie's heart leapt to her throat. "Who are you? How did you get in here?"

The figure stood silent and motionless. Then a horrible rasping voice issued from within its cowl: "You have disturbed powers beyond your comprehension. Now you shall face the consequences."

A blast of icy wind hurtled toward them, sending papers and debris swirling through the air. Jessie shrieked and grabbed George's arm as the occult artifacts began to rattle and shake. The chamber descended into chaos - a maelstrom of unseen forces bent on destruction.

Khan hissed at the air, trying in vain to ward off the malevolent spirit. But against this entity, even his supernatural abilities were no match.

They were no longer dealing with a mere ghost. An ancient and sinister magic had been unleashed upon them, and escape would not come easily...

Chapter 11

GEORGE AND JESSIE SUGGESTED to Bill Roberts that a case review would not go amiss as this was proving to be a complicated investigation. The Detective Sergeant readily agreed and suggested the meeting took place at their office in Dale Street. On querying this, Bill said he was being cautious because some of the guests at the garden party and murder suspects were influential people. He added, "Don't forget... Liverpool might be a city, but it is made up of many small villages."

During the case review, it was unanimously agreed that keeping an open mind was paramount and as a team they must consider all suspects. Leaning heavily on his experience as a detective, Bill reminded them to go through the guest list with a fine-tooth comb and do not ignore those on the list but failed to attend. That is what they did.

THE NEXT MORNING, JESSIE and George made their way to the home of Beatrice Smythe, Liverpool's most renowned psychic. According to Rosie's friends, Beatrice had predicted the murder a week before it happened. If there was any truth to her supposed abilities, she may provide a clue to help crack the case.

They found the old Victorian house shrouded in mystery, overgrown vines covering crumbling brickwork. A rusty gate creaked open to reveal a path winding through a tangled garden.

"Well, this looks suitably ominous," George remarked.

Jessie smiled. "Perfect setting for a psychic, don't you think?"

At their knock, the heavy oak door slowly opened. Before them stood a wisp of a woman, pale and ethereal in a flowing white dress. Her eyes were a piercing blue, gazing at them with a strange intensity.

"Welcome," she intoned in a soft, lilting voice. "I've been expecting you."

George raised a brow. "Have you now? And you are?"

"Beatrice Smythe. Please, come in." She stepped aside, gesturing them into a dimly lit foyer.

The interior of the house was as mysterious as its exterior. Heavy velvet curtains blocked the sunlight, candles flickered in polished sconces, the air thick with the scent of incense.

"Forgive the theatrics," Beatrice said, a wry twist to her lips. "Clients do expect a certain ambiance from their psychics."

"And do you truly have psychic abilities?" Jessie asked. "We understand you predicted Rosie O'Grady's murder."

A shadow passed over the woman's pale features. "Yes, I did foresee Rosie's tragic end. I tried to warn her, but she refused to listen." Beatrice sighed. "If only she had, perhaps her fate would have been different."

"In what way did you try to warn her?" George pressed. "What exactly did your vision show?"

Beatrice hesitated, her gaze turning inward. "Darkness," she whispered. "Danger all around. The raven, the wolf, the serpent..." She trailed off with a shudder.

"Symbols of death and deception," Jessie said. "It seems your vision indicated Rosie was surrounded by enemies. Do you have any sense of who these enemies might be?"

Beatrice shook her head. "The images were unclear. But there is great evil lurking here in Liverpool, and Rosie stumbled upon its path." Her eyes met Jessie's, pale blue eyes glowing with conviction. "You must be very careful, Miss Harper. Dark forces are at work, and they will stop at nothing to keep their secrets hidden."

A chill ran down Jessie's spine. This was more than theatrics—Beatrice genuinely seemed to believe her own words. But were her warnings mere speculation, or did she actually possess a gift of foresight?

One thing was clear: they had uncovered another piece of the puzzle. Rosie's murder was linked to secrets and dark forces, enemies who would kill to keep those secrets hidden. The mystery deepened, but Jessie was determined to see it through. She thanked Beatrice for her time and left the old house behind, Beatrice's unsettling words echoing in her mind.

JESSIE AND GEORGE MADE their way down the winding cobblestone lane toward Albert Humphries' dilapidated cottage. "Beatrice's warnings aside, we must not get carried away with speculation," George said. "We need facts, not fantastical tales of dark forces and hidden enemies."

"I understand your scepticism," Jessie replied. "But we cannot dismiss the possibility that Rosie stumbled upon something sinister. We must keep an open mind."

George sighed but did not argue further. They arrived at the cottage, the paint peeling and the yard overgrown with weeds. As they knocked on the weathered oak door, a strange menagerie of noises drifted through the walls—the chattering of monkeys, the hooting of owls, the growling of wild cats.

Albert Humphries answered the door in a flurry of feathers and fur. His coat was covered in white down and tufts of hair clung to his trousers. "What is it?" he snapped. "I'm very busy."

"Mr. Humphries, we're investigating the murder of Rosie O'Grady," Jessie said. "We understand you were acquainted with the victim."

"Knew her in passing," Albert muttered. He glanced over his shoulder, eyes shifting nervously. "Now if you'll excuse me, my work won't wait."

"Your work?" George peered around Albert's bulky form, catching a glimpse of movement inside. "Is that a monkey?"

Albert flushed, blocking the doorway. "That's none of your concern. Now off with you, I've no time for idle chit chat!" He slammed the door in their faces.

"Well, he was certainly acting suspicious," Jessie said. "And did you notice the strange noises we heard, and that brief sighting of a monkey? It seems Mr. Humphries' hobbies extend beyond taxidermy. We'll have to investigate further."

"Agreed," George said. "There is more to Mr. Humphries than meets the eye. He may well have motives for wanting Rosie out of the picture."

They continued down the lane, more determined than ever to uncover the truth. Rosie's killer was out there, lurking among the shadows, and Jessie had no intention of stopping until justice was served.

JESSIE PEERED OUT THE tram window as Liverpool's streets rolled by. "Next stop, the newspaper office. I want to have a word with Geraldine Finch."

George glanced up from his notebook. "The journalist who had an argument with Rosie at the garden party. What makes you suspect she's involved?"

"Her reaction seemed too vehement for a casual acquaintance," Jessie said. "And I didn't buy her explanation about Rosie causing a scene. There's more to their relationship than meets the eye."

"You think she may have been using the party to gather information for a story?" George asked.

"Precisely. Beatrice warned us that Rosie became obsessed with 'powers beyond her control.' If that's a reference to the occult practices of the secret society, it would make an intriguing expose."

The newspaper office was a bustle of activity, reporters shouting over the staccato rhythm of typewriters. Jessie approached the front desk and asked to speak with Geraldine Finch.

Moments later, a woman emerged from the chaos. She was tall and willowy, with a cap of glossy black curls and eyes as blue as cornflowers. "I'm Geraldine Finch. How may I help you?"

"I'm Jessie Harper, and this is my business associate George Jenkins," Jessie said. "We have some questions regarding your acquaintance with Rosie O'Grady."

Geraldine's polite smile faded. "Rosie O'Grady? I'm afraid I don't know anyone by that name."

"Really? That's not what you said at the party last week." Jessie studied her closely. "You seemed quite upset with her, in fact."

A flash of panic crossed the woman's face, swiftly hidden. "I apologize for the confusion, but I have never met anyone named Rosie O'Grady." She glanced at the clock. "Now if you'll excuse me, I have a deadline to meet."

"Not so fast," Jessie said. "I know you've been investigating the secret society Rosie was involved with. You can drop the act—we're aware of your undercover motives."

Geraldine paled but remained silent. Jessie had hit the mark.

"If Rosie discovered something that put her in danger, we need to know the truth," Jessie pressed. "Her life depended on it."

Geraldine looked away, a nerve in her jaw twitching. When she finally spoke, her voice was scarcely above a whisper. "I can't. If I reveal what I know...they'll kill me too."

Jessie's intuition tingled. There was more to this than meets the eye. She exchanged a glance with George, who gave a nearly imperceptible nod.

"We can protect you," Jessie said. "But if you don't cooperate, I'll have no choice but to expose your undercover operation. How did Rosie threaten to expose the society? What secret did she discover?"

Geraldine wrung her hands, eyes darting about the room. "I don't know the full details," she said at last. "Only that she claimed to have found an ancient artifact of great power, one the society has been searching for. She threatened to reveal its location if they didn't cease their criminal activities."

"An artifact?" Jessie's pulse quickened. "What kind of artifact?"

"I don't know, only that it's been hidden for centuries. Rosie said it contained knowledge that could destroy the society if exposed." Geraldine hesitated. "She was going to meet with a psychic to learn more about its whereabouts. A woman named..."

"Beatrice Smythe," Jessie finished. So, their hunch had been correct. The secret society had killed Rosie to protect some hidden treasure—and Beatrice likely knew far more than she had let on.

"Beatrice is involved with the society," Geraldine confirmed. "Rosie planned to get the information from her and then go public, exposing the society's corruption. But they must have found out. I tried to warn Rosie, but it was too late." Her eyes welled with tears. "I should have done more. Now an innocent woman is dead because of my cowardice."

"You did what you could," Jessie said. "Now you can make things right by helping us find justice for Rosie. Tell us everything you know about this artifact and the secret society. We'll handle the rest."

Geraldine took a steadying breath and nodded. "Very well. I'll tell you everything."

Geraldine's revelations about the secret society were chilling. Ritual sacrifices, blackmail, and political corruption reaching the highest levels of power—it was more sinister than Jessie could have imagined. But the most crucial piece of information was the artifact's location.

According to Geraldine, Rosie had discovered a cryptic map hidden in one of Albert Humphries' taxidermy pieces, pointing to an abandoned church in the countryside.

JESSIE AND GEORGE WASTED no time in searching Albert's house, and sure enough, they found the map tucked inside a hollowed-out badger. They had no problem locating the church. It was isolated, with a history of pagan worship dating back centuries. An ideal location to hide a valuable relic. As they approached along the winding country road, Jessie felt a surge of excitement and nerves. They were close—so close—to uncovering the truth and achieving justice for Rosie.

When they arrived, the church was dark and musty inside, cobwebs clinging to the rafters. But in a far corner, George let out a triumphant shout. "Look! There's a loose stone in the floor." He pried it open to reveal a hidden chamber below, and at the bottom, a wooden crate.

Heart pounding, Jessie descended into the chamber. She brushed away the layers of dust and debris to glimpse a metallic glint inside the crate—an ancient relic of ambiguous origin, just as Geraldine described.

She had found it. The secret society's coveted artifact, a piece of history that could expose their depravity and bring them to justice. Rosie's death would not be in vain.

At last, the truth was within their grasp. Jessie lifted the relic out of its chamber, ready to face the sinister forces that had tried to keep it hidden for so long. The secret society's reckoning was at hand.

Jessie and George looked at each other, determination etched into their expressions. They had the evidence they needed. Now it was time to confront the suspects with this new evidence.

FIRST ON THEIR LIST was Beatrice Smythe, the supposed psychic. When they arrived at her home, she greeted them with a smug smile, as if she already knew why they were there.

"So, you've found it, have you?" she purred. "The relic belongs to my coven. You have no right to take it."

"We know you and Rosie were rivals," Jessie said. "You wanted her out of the picture so you could have the relic for yourself."

Beatrice's composure faltered, and for a moment her facade of mystical wisdom faded, revealing a glimpse of spite. "Rosie was a thorn in my side. She stuck her nose where it didn't belong."

"And you had the motive and the means to kill her," George added. "Admit it—you were involved in her murder."

Beatrice's nostrils flared. "You have no proof. Now get out of my house before I curse you!"

They had rattled her, but she wasn't going to confess easily. On to the next suspect.

AT ALBERT HUMPHRIES'S ramshackle abode, the taxidermist was busy stuffing a fox, his hands slick with blood. "What do you want?" he grunted.

"We know you left clues to throw us off the trail," Jessie said. "But you're still a suspect. You killed Rosie to get the relic, didn't you? To add to your...collection." She grimaced at the lifeless animals surrounding them.

Albert paled. "I don't know what you're talking about."

"The map. The hidden chamber. It was all too convenient," George said. "Admit it—you killed Rosie to protect the relic."

Albert fumbled with his tools, dropping them to the floor. "I didn't kill anyone! Get out!"

Chapter 12

JESSIE BECAME OBSESSED with the thought there was still something they had all missed at the vicarage during the searches.

Entrusted with a key as an investigator, and anxious to prove her point, she stood in the dimly lit hallway of the vicarage, careful not to disturb the sleeping staff. Her heart raced as she glanced over her shoulder, checking for any signs of movement. The old floorboards creaked under her feet with each step as she made her way to the study.

She had to find any remaining evidence before they destroyed it. There was no time to lose.

The study door loomed before her, heavy oak that threatened to groan open and give her away at any moment. With a deep breath, she grasped the brass handle and eased the door open.

Silence greeted her. The room was empty.

Jessie stepped inside and pulled a small pocket torch from her handbag, clicking it on to scan the shelves and desk. Papers were strewn about haphazardly, drawers left open. Someone had already been here. Her chest tightened with frustration as she rummaged through the mess, overturning cushions and checking behind paintings.

There had to be something. Some small clue they had missed.

As she searched the desk, her torch glinted off a small object under the chair. Jessie dropped to her knees, peering into the shadows to get a better look. With a triumphant grin, she reached out and grabbed it, pulling it into the light. Her heart raced. She had found it.

False alarm! It was a small shard of glass no doubt the remnant of a brandy glass as she recalled a decanter on a small table close by.

Now, to get out of here without getting caught.

The floorboards creaked behind her. Jessie whipped around, but it was too late. A dark figure loomed in the doorway, candlestick raised and ready to strike.

Jessie stumbled back with a gasp as the figure lunged toward her, candlestick swinging through the air. She raised her arms to shield herself, bracing for the blow—

"Jessie! It's me, George!"

She blinked, peering through her arms at the familiar voice. George stood before her, candlestick in hand and eyes wide with alarm.

Jessie exhaled in relief, lowering her arms. "George! You nearly frightened me out of my wits. What are you doing here?"

"I could ask you the same thing," he said, eyeing the torch in her hand. "I thought I heard noises coming from the vicarage and came to investigate. Imagine my surprise finding you rummaging through the Reverend's desk in the dead of night!"

"It's not what it looks like," Jessie insisted. "I admit I do have a bee in my bonnet that we have missed a vital clue and that's why I decided to come here alone in the dead of the night."

"Dead!" George snorted; the only thing dead will be you if you sneak off without telling me. We are partners, don't forget that."

"George, I am sorry. You are right... but may I ask why you are also here in the dead of the night."

"You may. I also had a bee in my bonnet that one or more of our suspects would return to the scene of the crime, so I hid near to the garden."

"Without telling me!" Jessie laughed.

George laughed too but soon recovered his composure and placing his index finger against his lips, he whispered, "Let's go. We are acting like foolish amateurs. I think we need to get back to the office and thrash out the next steps in this complicated investigation.

THE REMAINDER OF THE night was long and sleep eluded Jessie. Her mind raced with images of all the suspects, actual and possible, replaying each clue and conversation that had led them to this point in the investigation.

When dawn finally broke, pale light filtering through the curtains, Jessie rose with a weary sigh. She had resolved to face this day and following days head-on, dangers be damned. There would be no rest, no refuge until the murderer was behind bars.

Jessie heard a knock on her bedroom door then George asked, "Time for breakfast?"

"Coming," Jessie said as she threw on her robe. Making her way to the small kitchen table, she saw dark circles hanging under his eyes, betraying a sleepless night of his own.

Over toast and tea, they plotted their next move. "I do think we need to speak to the main suspects again, don't you?" George said.

"I do because we don't seem to have go very far with any of them and besides, we need to keep up the pressure by reminding them we aren't going away," Jessie said.

"Yes. Perhaps one of them will crack if we keep at them asking questions and generally being an unwanted presence in their lives," George added.

Breakfast over, George meandered down to the street entrance to the office to check if any post had arrived. There was but he left opening it until both he and Jessie had bathed and dressed ready for another day's work.

He opened the first envelope noticing it bore no postmark but thought nothing of it for often people dropped off letters of all kinds in person rather than use the post office.

The anonymous threat arrived on a crisp white card, its bold black letters slicing into Jessie's calm with the precision of a stiletto. George handed it to Jessie. She traced a finger over the ominous words, dread pooling in her stomach. *Abandon the investigation—or suffer the consequences.*

"It seems our villain has a flair for the dramatic," George said, peering over her shoulder. His tone was light, but she detected the tension in his voice. They both knew this was no idle threat.

Jessie swallowed against the bitter taste in her mouth and forced a smile. "And a fondness for stationery. At least they have good penmanship."

George gave her arm an approving squeeze, his weathered face creasing into a smile. "That's the spirit, Jessie. We won't give them the satisfaction of rattling us."

"You're right, of course." She squared her shoulders and met his gaze, determination flooding her senses. "This changes nothing. We press on."

Khan let out an approving meow from his spot by the fireplace, his luminous green eyes gleaming with purpose.

Jessie strode to her desk and pinned the note to a cork board, joining the web of clues they had gathered so far. "Now, let's think. What does this tell us about our villain?"

"For one, they don't want us digging into the society's past," George said. "There's something there they don't want uncovered."

"Precisely." Jessie tapped the note with a finger. "And they're watching us closely enough to know we're getting close to the truth."

"Close enough to worry them, at any rate." George limped to stand beside her, surveying their collection of clues. "The question is, what are they planning to do about it?"

A chill ran down Jessie's spine as she considered the implications. This was no longer a simple case of solving a murder. They were now engaged in a dangerous game of cat and mouse—and the stakes had never been higher.

She stared at the web of clues, searching for the pattern that would reveal their adversary, her mind whirling with questions and half-formed theories. Somewhere in this tangled mess was the key to unmasking a killer.

Jessie simply had to find it before the villain made another move. The game was certainly afoot.

Jessie paced the length of her office, pausing every so often to glance at the clues tacked to her cork board. Somewhere within that tangled web was the answer, if only she could see it.

Khan leapt onto the windowsill, his green eyes following her movements. "You're missing something, aren't you?"

She sighed, raking a hand through her hair. "Yes. Something obvious that I should have seen by now."

"The villain didn't leave us much to go on with that note. No fingerprints. No signature. Just a scrap of paper with a hastily scrawled message." Khan flicked his tail, a sure sign he was pondering the mystery. "So, what does that tell us?"

"That they're careful. Meticulous, even." Jessie frowned, circling the desk to stand before the cork board once more. "Everything they've done so far has been calculated and precise."

"Except for one thing." Khan's eyes gleamed with realization. "The garden party. That was sloppy."

Jessie's eyes widened. "You're right. Killing Rosie in front of all those witnesses...that was reckless. Out of character for someone so careful in their planning."

"And why did they do it?" Khan prompted. "What was the motive behind such a brazen act?"

The pieces snapped into place like the final strokes of a masterful portrait. Jessie turned to George, a triumphant smile spreading across her face.

"I've solved it! I know who killed Rosie O'Grady."

George set down his cup of tea. "Well, don't keep me in suspense! Who is our murderer?"

Jessie began to pace, her mind racing. "Rosie O'Grady was killed in front of witnesses for a reason. The murderer wanted us to assume it was a crime of passion, a reckless act fuelled by jealousy or rage."

"But you don't believe that." George leaned forward, intrigued.

"No. Our murderer is too careful, too calculating for that. Everything up until now has been meticulously planned." Jessie paused, meeting his gaze. "Except the garden party. That was staged to throw us off the scent. Rosie O'Grady was murdered in cold blood, not out of passion or impulse."

"So, the killer wanted us to suspect someone with a grudge against Rosie," George reasoned. "Someone who appeared to have motive and opportunity in front of all those witnesses."

"Exactly." Jessie nodded. "And there's only one person who benefits from us suspecting a crime of passion."

"The real murderer," George finished. "Someone who wanted to direct our attention away from them. But who?"

Jessie smiled, savouring the final revelation. "The one person we least suspected. The one person no one would believe capable of such a heinous act."

She paused for effect, watching as the pieces fell into place behind George's eyes. His face paled, his mouth falling open in disbelief.

"You can't mean..." He shook his head, stunned. "Surely not..."

"I'm afraid so." Jessie's gaze hardened with grim determination. "The villain isn't one of the guests at all. In fact, the killer has been right under our noses this whole time."

George stared at her, incredulous. "But how? It's simply not possible."

"Oh, but it is." Jessie's lips curled into a mirthless smile. "While we were busy suspecting the others, the killer was watching. Waiting. Calculating their next move."

She sighed, rubbing her temples. The pieces of the puzzle were finally coming together, but the truth was almost too much to bear. How could they have been so blind?

"The threat, the attacks, the traps..." George's voice trailed off as the implications sank in. He shook his head again, slower this time, and when he looked at Jessie again there was a shadow of fear in his eyes. "All this time, we were in danger. From the very person we trusted most."

Jessie nodded grimly. "The killer wanted us to abandon the investigation. What better way than to make us live in fear, looking over our shoulder with every step? It was the perfect way to distract us, to weaken our resolve."

"And it almost worked," George said softly. "I nearly convinced you to give up, to leave this place once and for all." His face twisted in anguish and regret. "If I had succeeded..."

"Don't dwell on it." Jessie grasped his hands, her tone gentle yet firm. "We're on to them now. And we won't stop until we've uncovered the truth and brought Rosie's killer to justice."

She squeezed his hands, feeling the familiar warmth and steadfastness that had drawn her to him from the start. "Together, we're stronger. Together, we will prevail."

George's expression softened, the shadows in his eyes fading into quiet determination. He smiled and gave her hands a reassuring squeeze in return.

"Together," he echoed firmly. "We will bring this villain down."

Again, Jessie surveyed the clues laid out before them on the office wall. Photographs of the crime scene, transcripts of interviews, receipts and invoices, everything they had gathered so far in their investigation.

"There must be something here we've missed," she muttered, brows knitting in frustration. "Some small detail that ties it all together."

George leaned back in his chair, steepling his fingers as he studied the array of evidence. "The killer wanted to throw us off their scent.

So, they would plant false clues to distract us, send us down the wrong path."

"Misdirection," Jessie said with a nod. "To conceal the truth in plain sight. We need to look past the obvious, find what doesn't quite fit."

"Motive, means and opportunity," George said. "We know the killer had means and opportunity. Now we must discern their motive, the reason behind these murders."

"Revenge," Jessie said slowly. "Retribution for some perceived wrong. But who had reason to resent Rosie so deeply?"

"The secret society," George said. "There were rumours of a rift within its ranks, a betrayal of trust that tore the group apart."

Jessie's eyes widened. "Of course. One of the society's own members, driven by bitterness and a desire for vengeance against those they believed had wronged them."

"We've been looking in the wrong places," George said grimly. "The killer was hiding in plain sight, masquerading as an ally while plotting their revenge."

Jessie stared at the clues with renewed purpose, searching for the missing piece that would reveal the killer's identity at last. "Now we know where to look. And this time, we'll catch them in the act."

Chapter 13

JESSIE SIFTED THROUGH the letters and documents, looking for any hint of resentment or animosity. There. A faint crease in the corner of an old photograph, as if crumpled in anger. She examined it closely and gasped.

The photo showed Rosie and four others in front of an old manor, smiling brightly for the camera. But one face had been viciously scratched out, the eyes gouged away in a display of rage.

"George, look at this," Jessie said, handing him the photo. "Rosie and the others, all except..."

"The colonel," George breathed. "Colonel Windsor, their former leader according to gossip. It seems he may have harboured a grudge against Rosie and the rest of the group for expelling him."

Jessie nodded, a chill running down her spine. "And now he's picking them off one by one, driven by vengeance to destroy everything they built."

Khan leapt onto the table, peering at the photo. "This is bad. Very bad. The colonel was always unstable, but if he's truly behind these murders, he won't stop until you're all dead."

"We have to find him first," Jessie said. "Before he strikes again."

Just then a loud crash of shattered glass broke the silence. Jessie ran down the stairs to the street entrance to find a brick lying amidst the glass remains of the outer front door, a scrap of paper tied around it.

She unfurled the note with trembling fingers as George watched on.

Last warning. Back off now or suffer the consequences. You've been warned.

George's face was ashen. "It seems we've angered the beast. The killer knows we're getting close. And now he's coming after us."

The villain was no longer content to toy with them, striking from the shadows. This was a direct threat, brazen and unhinged. Jessie felt a chill of dread. They were all in terrible danger, caught in a deadly game with a cunning and ruthless adversary who would stop at nothing to defeat them. The stakes had never been higher, and one wrong move could cost them everything.

Jessie's pulse raced as she surveyed the damage. She felt they were running out of time. The killer was poised to strike again, and they were woefully unprepared. She turned to George, her eyes hard with resolve. "We need help. Call Bill - tell him it's an emergency."

George nodded and rushed to the phone as Jessie began boarding up the broken glass. Within minutes, the familiar rumble of Bill's voice came rolling up the stairs.

"Up here." George said.

Entering the office, Bill took one look at the brick and note and swore under his breath. "This has gone too far, Jessie. You're not equipped to handle a threat like this."

"We have no choice," Jessie said. "The killer, and we think it's Colonel Windsor, won't stop until he's destroyed us. Our only hope is to find him first."

Bill studied her for a long moment, his craggy face creased with concern. But Jessie could see he understood - they couldn't back down now. Finally, he sighed and scrubbed a hand over his face. "Right. We need a plan."

"We've been going about this all wrong," Jessie said. "Windsor doesn't want us searching records or asking questions. He wants to throw us off the scent. So, we need to change tactics - go to the last place he'd expect."

"The society," George said, eyes lighting with realization. "He'd never believe we'd look there. Not after all these years."

A grim smile tugged at Jessie's lips. "Exactly. It's time we paid a visit to the Inner Circle."

Bill frowned. "But how? That old manor house has been abandoned for some time. There's no way in, and even if there was, the clues we need could be anywhere."

"Not anywhere," Jessie said. "There's one place Windsor would keep records, plans, anything that could incriminate him. The Master's study."

Comprehension dawned on George's face. "Where the leader of the Inner Circle would meet. Hold all their secrets. If there's evidence to find, that's where it will be."

"But the study was sealed off," Bill said. "No one's been inside for years."

"No one except the colonel," Jessie said. "He may have covered his tracks, but there will be signs. We just have to look closely enough."

Bill eyed them for a long moment, resignation etching lines in his face. But they could see he knew it was their best chance. This was a risk, but if they played their cards right, it could lead them straight to the killer's door. The villain had made a mistake, and now it was time to make him pay.

THEY ARRIVED AT THE abandoned Inner Circle estate under cover of night, flashlights flickering over crumbling stone walls and cobwebbed windows. An owl hooted softly in the distance, the only sound in this place of decaying secrets.

Jessie shone her light over an ornate wooden door, dust-covered but intact. "The Master's study. This is our way in." She tried the handle and found it locked, as expected. "George, if you would?"

George kneeled beside the lock, tools at the ready. His dexterous fingers probed the mechanism, and within minutes there was a satisfying click.

The study was dim and musty, frozen in time. But signs of recent disturbance caught Jessie's eye at once. Faint footprints in the dust, a few objects out of place. "The colonel has been here. And recently."

Bill grunted. "How can you be sure?"

"The dust is undisturbed elsewhere. These prints are fresh. And look-" She crossed to an oak desk and pulled out a drawer. "These papers have been rifled through."

"What are they?" George asked, peering over her shoulder.

"Membership lists, by the look of it." Jessie's heart raced as she sorted through the pages. Any clue, any thread they could follow...

There. Two names, underscored in red ink. Ellen and Joyce Rosie O'Grady. And next to it, a sinister note in a jagged hand: *Danger. Silence them.*

"He's marked the sisters for death," Jessie breathed. "Rosie's daughters are in danger. We have to warn them, now!"

Bill blanched. "You're right. And there's something else." He stabbed a finger at the bottom of the page. "Look at the date. These notes were made just days ago. He is planning to strike soon."

Jessie's hands clenched around the brittle paper, rage and fear mingling in her gut. They had found his Achilles heel, but now the villain was poised to lash out. The hunt had just become a race against time.

Chapter 14

JOYCE O'GRADY OPENED the door after she heard the frantic knocking. She was relieved to see it was Jessie for her heart was pounding thinking the worst.

"Joyce! We have to talk, now!"

Ellen emerged from the sitting room, her usually cheerful face creasing in concern. "Jessie? What on earth's the matter?"

"You're both in danger," Jessie said bluntly. "We believe Colonel Windsor has marked you for death. We found notes planning to 'silence' you."

The girls' face drained of colour. "No. Not now, not when you told us you are so close..."

"We think he means to strike soon." Jessie grasped the girls' hands. "You can't stay here. Come back to the vicarage with us, Reverend Bennett will keep you safe."

"We can't run from him forever," Ellen said softly. "And if we hide, he wins." A determined gleam lit her eyes. "We need to set a trap."

"Too risky," George warned. "He's desperate. He won't give you a fighting chance."

"All the more reason to stop running and face him once and for all." Joyce smiled grimly. "With all of you by my side, we have strength in numbers. Let's give him a taste of his own medicine."

Jessie glanced at George, seeing her own resolve reflected in his face. Joyce was right. This was their chance to confront the villain and end his reign of terror, once and for all.

"We're with you," Jessie said. "Just tell us what you have in mind."

Joyce nodded, "Here's the plan..."

JESSIE'S HEART POUNDED as she crept through the abandoned factory. Somewhere in this maze of shadows and cobwebs lurked the colonel waiting to spring his trap.

She clutched her torch tightly, ready to use it as a weapon, straining her ears for any sound. The villain had gone eerily silent after his last taunting message. The calm before the storm.

A floorboard creaked behind her. Jessie whirled, her torch beam illuminating the darkness. A scream rang out—Joyce or Ellen had clearly hit their mark.

The colonel stumbled into view, clutching his bruised and bleeding head. "Clever girl," he rasped. "But not clever enough."

He lunged at her with a knife. Jessie dodged but tripped on the uneven floor. The colonel seized her arm, twisting it cruelly. She cried out, dropping her torch.

"At last, I have you," Colonel Windsor gloated. "Time to end this tiresome game." He raised the knife, eyes glinting with madness.

A gunshot rang out. Windsor shrieked, the knife falling from his grasp. He crumpled to the floor, revealing George standing behind him, smoking pistol in hand.

"Game over," George said grimly. He rushed to help Jessie up as Bill Roberts and two constables came running in.

"George told me about the plan. I didn't like it one bit so decided to come here under my own steam." Bill panted. "What you didn't know is that the colonel is not the killer."

"Really?" Jessie said looking sheepish.

"Yes, really. He left a note that contained many threats because he was angry about being kicked out of the secret society's top echelon. He no longer had any power. There is no evidence at all he was responsible for Rosie's murder nor any involvement with the art heist. Indeed, he stated that in his note and I believe him."

"At least Joyce and Ellen can sleep easy in their own beds again," George said.

"Indeed, Constable will you take Joyce and Ellen with you and make sure they get home safe and sound," Bill said. Waiting until the girls were out of earshot, Bill continued, "Jessie, George, never do anything like that again. It was foolish and dangerous and all because one of those girls suggested the plan. My experience tells me that one of your other suspects is the real killer. I suggest you go and interview them yet again."

"We plan to do that," Jessie said.

"Well, bloody well do it and pardon my French, Miss Harper," Bill snapped. "This is not the library. This is the real world where people get killed by bad people."

Bill turned on his heels leaving George and Jessie to reflect on this harsh lesson.

Jessie clasped George's hand, relief washing over her. "We still make a good team."

George smiled. "Partners to the end."

Chapter 15

"DETECTIVE SERGEANT Roberts reporting, sirs," began the account, as I stood before my superiors in the headquarters' cramped conference room. "The investigation into the murder at the vicarage has taken numerous twists and turns, with Jessie Harper and George Jenkins of Dale Street Private Investigations presenting shifting theories that have led to a convoluted set of clues."

"Upon further analysis of the crime scene," I continued, using the terse police jargon I knew my audience appreciated, "previously overlooked details have come to light, including potential evidence pointing to various suspects. However, these newfound clues have also presented red herrings, complicated our assessment and forced us to continually revise our hypotheses."

"Jessie and George's adaptability and resilience in the face of these puzzling developments has been invaluable," I emphasized. "They've navigated dead-end leads and frustrating inconsistencies, all while questioning their interpretations of the evidence and recalibrating their views on the potential suspects."

"Throughout the investigation, several theories and initial suspects have been discarded," I said, making sure to use the official terminology to describe the process. "This continual refinement of our suspect pool has brought us closer to unveiling the true culprit."

"Recently, Jessie and George discovered unexpected connections between some of the key players in this case," I informed them. "These new insights have reshaped our approach, challenging our original ideas about motives and alibis."

"Despite the numerous setbacks and frustrations, Jessie and George have shown unwavering commitment to solving this case," I stressed, commending their perseverance. "The emotional toll of such an investigation is not lost on us, but they continue to push forward, understanding that only through persistence will the truth be uncovered."

"Through diligent analysis, Jessie and George have recently uncovered a critical piece of evidence that was previously overlooked. This revelatory moment has prompted them to revisit earlier theories and reinterpret the evidence in a new light."

"Following this breakthrough, Jessie and George have formulated a groundbreaking theory that brings them closer to the truth," I concluded, describing the climactic shift in the investigation. "With newfound direction and dedication, they will follow this lead, inching ever closer to unmasking the killer."

As I finished my report, the room was silent for a moment before my superiors began discussing the details of the case, their voices laden with anticipation. It was clear that the peculiarities of this investigation had captured their attention, and as they delved deeper into the intricacies of the case, there was a shared understanding that we were on the precipice of solving this enigmatic murder.

"However," Sergeant Roberts continued, his voice taking on a more sombre tone, "it's not all smooth sailing for our intrepid duo. They've encountered their fair share of roadblocks and red herrings, as is to be expected in such an intricate case."

"Tell me more about these challenges," Chief Inspector Thompson prompted, his brow furrowing in concern.

"Of course, sir," Roberts replied, riffling through his notes to locate the pertinent information. "Jessie and George have faced several instances of dead-end leads, leaving them to retrace their steps and reassess the situation. For instance, they pursued one line of inquiry that cantered around a suspicious message received by the victim just hours before her demise. Regrettably, it turned out to be a false lead, as the message was later deemed inconsequential."

"Ah, a classic red herring," Thompson remarked with a knowing nod.

"Indeed, sir," Roberts agreed. "But it doesn't end there. The inconsistencies in witness testimonies have only served to further complicate matters. It appears that certain individuals have motivations to obfuscate the truth, causing Jessie and George to expend valuable time and resources untangling the web of deception."

"Quite frustrating, I imagine," Thompson interjected, his empathy for the detectives' plight evident in his expression.

"Extremely so, sir," Roberts confirmed. "Yet Jessie and George refuse to let these setbacks deter them. They've learned to question their initial conclusions, embracing the reality that their initial assumptions might not always hold water. In fact, Jessie has developed quite the knack for sifting through the chaff to uncover the precious kernels of truth."

"An invaluable skill in this line of work," Thompson mused aloud, admiration clear in his voice.

"Absolutely, sir," Roberts concurred. "And despite the roadblocks and red herrings they've encountered, Jessie and George remain steadfast in their pursuit of the truth. Their determination to uncover the identity of the killer has only grown stronger in the face of adversity."

"Excellent," Thompson declared, his eyes filled with renewed confidence in the abilities of the investigating duo. "I have no doubt that Jessie and George will overcome these challenges and bring this confounding case to a satisfying conclusion."

"Neither do I, sir," Roberts affirmed, the conviction in his voice unwavering. "Rest assured that they'll leave no stone unturned in their quest for justice."

"Very well, Sergeant," Thompson concluded, offering a nod of approval. "Keep me updated on their progress and let me know if any further assistance is needed."

"Will do, sir, especially the latest information that the deceased may have had some involvement in that big art heist a few years go."

"Hmm, interesting, Sergeant."

"Quite so," Roberts responded as he gathered his notes and prepared to take his leave. "You can count on us."

Chapter 16

ON THE NIGHT OF THE debacle with Colonel Windsor, George and Jessie had told Bill Roberts that they had planned to interview the suspects again. It was true.

George paced back and forth in their office, the worn-out wooden floorboards creaking under his weight. To his annoyance, sometimes the tip of his cane would become stuck between small gaps between the boards. Photos, newspaper clippings, and scribbled notes were spread all over the desk, a mosaic of clues and connections. Jessie sat on the other side, her fingers drumming on the armrest of her chair, her gaze distant and contemplative.

"I know we have said this before but we're missing something, Jessie," George muttered, halting to look at the wall of connections they had built over the past month. Strings connected pictures, forming a web of relationships and interactions.

Jessie sighed, rubbing her tired eyes. "It sometimes feels like we've interviewed nearly half the village. Everyone's a suspect in their own way. But these small leads, they're distractions. We're getting lost."

George nodded, "You're right. It's time to go back to basics, to our main suspects. No more wild goose chases."

"Yes, and Bill's advice to a tee so let's do it and show him we are up to the task in hand," Jessie said.

The two had been working on the murder case with its connections to an art heist. The list of suspects wasn't too long, with various motivations and alibis. But amongst them, three stood out: Beatrice Smythe, the psychic, Albert Humphries, the taxidermist, and Geraldine Finch, the reporter.

"It's one of them," George said, picking up the photos of the three suspects. "We need to look closely, interrogate them again, and watch for any slip, any inconsistency."

Jessie nodded, "I've been thinking about Geraldine. There's something about her story that doesn't add up. She claimed she didn't meet Rosie at the garden party but we know that's a lie."

"And Albert," George interjected, "He's slippery. I'm convinced he knows something. But we need more than just a gut feeling. We need concrete evidence."

"There's also the psychic, Beatrice Smythe," Jessie said, leaning forward. "She's been evasive since day one. I think it's time we press harder. We need to shake her up, make her spill."

George looked at Jessie, a determination in his eyes. "No more distractions. We concentrate on these three. One of them is our killer."

Jessie gathered the relevant files and stood up, her resolve clear. "Let's start with Beatrice. She's got secrets, that one. We need to catch her off guard."

The two detectives left the office with renewed energy, knowing they had a direction to follow. The village's secrets were deep, but George and Jessie were certain. Behind one of those innocent faces lay the mind of a cunning killer. And they were just a few steps away from unveiling the truth.

"George, I believe it's time we divide and conquer," Jessie declared, her eyes sparkling with determination. "I shall pay a visit to Beatrice Smythe for further inquiries. Perhaps you could follow up on Albert Humphries?"

"An excellent idea, Miss Harper," George agreed, adjusting his tweed jacket. "We must leave no stone unturned in this investigation."

"Then it's settled," Jessie said, nodding resolutely. "Khan, would you accompany me to see Beatrice?"

"Of course, Jessie," Khan replied, his green eyes gleaming mysteriously. "I am always at your service."

"Good luck, both of you," George said before parting ways. "And remember, trust no one but each other."

"Be safe, George" Jessie called after him, her heart swelling with gratitude for their makeshift alliance.

AFTER CONSULTING WITH Detective Sergeant Roberts, Bill agreed that it was better for George to interview Albert Humphries at the police station to try and place more pressure on the taxidermist. Accordingly, George telephoned the suspect and made it clear that the invitation to attend the interview was not one to be declined.

"Albert, have a seat," George said, gesturing to a chair in the bare interview room at Hatton Garden police station. The shadows cast by a flickering overhead light bulb danced across the walls, lending an air of intrigue to their meeting.

"Thank you, Mr. Jenkins," Albert replied, his voice wavering slightly as he took a seat. "I must say, I'm rather surprised to find myself here."

"Surprised? Why is that?" George asked, settling into a chair opposite him and observing Albert with keen interest.

"Because I am quite aware of your recent investigations," Albert said, wringing his hands nervously. "And although I have nothing to hide, it's disquieting to be the subject of such scrutiny."

"Understandable," George acknowledged. "But I assure you, we're simply trying to get to the bottom of this unfortunate business."

"Of course," Albert murmured, avoiding George's gaze. "What do you wish to know?"

"Let's start with your past, shall we?" George suggested, his tone firm but not unkind. "You were accused of a similar crime many years ago, were you not?"

"Indeed," Albert admitted, his face flushing with shame. "But let me be clear, I was never convicted due to lack of evidence. It was all just a terrible misunderstanding."

"Be that as it may," George said, leaning forward in his chair. "Can you think of any reason why someone would want to dredge up your past now?"

"None whatsoever," Albert replied, his voice barely audible. "I've tried my best to put those dark days behind me."

"Perhaps someone is trying to frame you," George mused, watching Albert closely for any sign of deception.

"Frame me? But why?" Albert asked, his brow furrowed with confusion.

"Ah, that's the question, isn't it?" George replied, tapping his fingers on the armrest. "It seems someone is going to great lengths to mislead us."

"Who would do such a thing?" Albert inquired, genuine fear creeping into his voice.

"I wish I knew," George confessed, his mind racing with possibilities. "But rest assured, we will not stop until we uncover the truth."

"Thank you, Mr. Jenkins," Albert said, his shoulders sagging with relief. "I only hope that the truth comes to light before any more harm is done."

"Indeed," George agreed, rising from his chair. "For all our sakes. You are free to go but please make sure I can be in touch with you in case there are fresh developments."

George couldn't quite put his finger on it but in that moment, he felt they were inching closer to the truth, but the path ahead was still fraught with deception and danger. And yet, he was determined to press on, trusting in their collective instincts and the bonds forged between Jessie, Khan, and himself. The mystery continued to deepen, and the stakes had never been higher.

AS JESSIE APPROACHED the residence of Beatrice Smythe, she couldn't help but feel a sense of trepidation. There was something unsettling about the woman, a vague malevolence that seemed to emanate from her very being. But Jessie was not one to shy away from danger; she knew that solving this mystery would require facing the unknown head-on.

"Are you ready, Khan?" Jessie asked, stealing a glance at the black cat by her side.

"Always, Jessie" he responded, his voice steady and reassuring.

Jessie took a deep breath, squared her shoulders, and knocked on the door. The sound echoed ominously through the house, sending shivers down her spine. After a tense moment, the door creaked open to reveal Beatrice Smythe herself.

"Ah, Miss Harper, what a surprise" Beatrice greeted her, her voice dripping with false warmth. "To what do I owe the pleasure?"

"Mrs. Smythe, I have a few more questions regarding the recent events" Jessie began, her tone firm yet polite. "May I come in?"

"Very well" Beatrice acquiesced, stepping aside to allow Jessie and Khan entry into her home.

As they stepped over the threshold, Jessie couldn't help but notice an odd sensation, as if the very air within the house was charged with energy. She shook off the feeling and focused her attention on Beatrice.

"Mrs. Smythe, I must be frank" Jessie said, fixing the woman with a piercing gaze. "There are certain aspects of your story that simply do not add up."

"Is that so?" Beatrice replied, her eyes narrowing ever so slightly.

"Indeed" Jessie continued, her resolve unwavering. "I suspect there is more to this than meets the eye, and I intend to uncover the truth."

"Miss Harper, you may find that the truth is not always what we wish it to be" Beatrice warned, her voice taking on a dangerous edge.

"Nevertheless" Jessie countered, meeting Beatrice's stare without flinching, "it is my duty to seek it out, no matter where it leads."

"Very well" Beatrice conceded, a cold smile playing across her lips. "Ask your questions, Miss Harper. But remember, once the truth is revealed, there is no going back."

Jessie nodded, steeling herself for the confrontation ahead. With Khan by her side, she would face the darkness and bring the truth to light, whatever the cost. For the sake of their community and their own lives, failure was simply not an option.

"Miss Smythe, you were acquainted with the deceased, correct?" asked Jessie, her palms resting on the edge of the table between them.

"Of course," Beatrice replied, a nonchalant wave of her hand dismissing the question as inconsequential. "Our circles did overlap, after all."

Jessie's brow furrowed, her eyes never leaving Beatrice's face. Khan, meanwhile, had positioned himself near the window, carefully observing the psychic while remaining out of her line of sight. As if sensing his presence, Beatrice shivered involuntarily, casting a wary glance in the direction of the seemingly empty space.

"Jessie," Khan whispered so only she could hear, "there's something... off about this woman. Be cautious."

"Indeed, Mrs. Smythe" Jessie continued, her voice steady. "But it seems that you've neglected to mention certain details regarding your relationship with the victim."

"Such as?" Beatrice inquired, feigning ignorance.

"Your recent falling out" Jessie responded candidly, watching as Beatrice's mask of indifference wavered ever so slightly. "It's rather curious, wouldn't you say?"

"Curious, perhaps" Beatrice admitted, her grip tightening around the porcelain teacup cradled in her hands. "But irrelevant" she added, emphasizing the word with an air of finality.

"Is it, though?" Jessie mused aloud, her gaze unyielding. "I find it hard to believe that such animosity would have no bearing on the matter at hand."

"Miss Harper" Beatrice began, her voice tinged with impatience, "I assure you that my personal affairs have no connection to this unfortunate incident."

"Perhaps" Jessie conceded, though her expression betrayed her lingering doubts. "But it is my responsibility to determine whether that is indeed the case."

"Very well" Beatrice sighed, her voice laced with a hint of resignation. "Proceed with your line of questioning" she added, though her eyes betrayed a flicker of unease.

"Thank you" Jessie said firmly, ready to delve deeper into the matter at hand. But as she began to formulate her next question, her thoughts were interrupted by a sudden commotion outside the window.

"Miss Harper" Khan hissed urgently, his tail twitching in agitation. "I believe George may have uncovered something important" he added, his ears perked in the direction of the noise.

"Excuse me" Jessie said hastily, rising from her chair and turning towards the door. "But I must see to a pressing matter" she explained, leaving Beatrice sitting alone at the table.

"Of course," Beatrice replied, her expression unreadable as she watched Jessie's retreating figure.

As Jessie exited the house, she found George waiting for her on the sidewalk, his face flushed and his eyes wide with alarm.

"Jessie" he panted, out of breath from his hurried arrival. "I've just come from the police station after interviewing Albert Humphries," he explained, struggling to catch his breath.

"George" Jessie urged, her concern evident in her tone. "What did you learn?"

"Jessie" George stammered, his voice barely above a whisper. "Albert was accused of a similar crime years ago" he revealed, his eyes darting nervously around them as if fearing eavesdroppers. "There wasn't enough evidence to convict him" he continued. his voice hushed but urgent. "But it raises some serious questions" he added, his gaze meeting Jessie's with an intensity that spoke volumes.

"Indeed" Jessie murmured, her mind racing with the implications of this new information. "We'll need to tread carefully" she warned, her eyes narrowing in determination. "Nothing is as it seems" she added, her voice barely audible as she glanced back towards Beatrice's house, a shiver running down her spine as the gravity of their situation began to sink in.

"Let us retire to the office," Jessie declared, her eyes alight with determination. "We must collate our findings and see what connections we can discern between Beatrice and Albert."

"Agreed," George nodded, his brow furrowed in thought. They made their way through the streets, the weight of the information they had uncovered heavy on their minds.

AS THEY SETTLED INTO their chairs, Jessie recounted Khan's observations, the subtle flick of his tail and the twitch of his ear as he scrutinized Beatrice. Her voice was low, yet animated, as she described the strange energy that seemed to emanate from the psychic during their encounter.

"Curious," George mused, rubbing his chin. "And if it is true that Albert was accused of a similar crime before, could there be some connection between him and Beatrice?"

"Indeed," Jessie nodded, her eyes narrowing as she considered the possibilities. "But we must not allow ourselves to be led astray. There is a malignant force at work here, I am certain of it."

"Quite so," George affirmed, his expression sombre. "We shall have to be vigilant and trust in our instincts."

"Tomorrow, we shall delve deeper into this mystery" Jessie announced, her voice resolute. "But for now, let us retire and gather our strength for the challenges ahead."

Chapter 17

THE FOLLOWING DAY, Jessie found herself on familiar ground - outside the library where she used to work, lost in thought as she contemplated their investigation. Khan, ever the faithful companion, trotted beside her, his keen gaze never straying far from her side.

"Look here" Jessie murmured, bending down to pick up a box that lay discarded near the entrance. It contained a small, twisted object. It was an ornate silver mirror, its tarnished surface clouded and warped. Jessie believed she had seen such a mirror listed as one of the stolen items from the art heist at the nearby art gallery. There was also a business card bearing the name of Beatrice Smythe, renowned psychic.

"Khan" she whispered, her voice tinged with apprehension. "Could this be the work of Beatrice?"

The cat studied the object intently, his ears twitching as he considered its potential significance. "It is possible" he conceded, his voice low and guarded. "But we must not jump to conclusions."

"Indeed" Jessie agreed, her expression thoughtful. "This seems almost too convenient" she mused, her eyes narrowing in suspicion. "As though someone wishes us to believe that Beatrice is responsible."

"Perhaps" Khan replied, his whiskers quivering with unease. "But we must tread carefully" he cautioned, his tail flicking restlessly behind him. "There may be darker forces at play here than we can yet comprehend."

"Quite" Jessie nodded, her heart heavy with the knowledge that their investigation was far from over. "We shall proceed with caution" she vowed, her grip tightening around the mysterious mirror as they made their way back to their office, each step bringing them closer to the truth that lay hidden in the shadows.

GEORGE, STILL PONDERING Jessie's suspicions about the evidence found near the library, felt a chill run down his spine as he noticed a constable in uniform approaching him. There was something about the officer's demeanour that set George on edge.

"Ah, Mr. Jenkins," the officer began, extending a folder towards George. "I wonder if you might be able to shed some light on this."

"Do we know one another?" George said.

"Sorry, we do. We met briefly at the crime scene. I am Constable Walker."

George hesitated for a moment before taking the proffered folder. As he opened it and scanned the contents, his brow furrowed in genuine puzzlement. The folder contained what appeared to be incriminating evidence linking Jessie to the crime they were investigating. He looked up at Officer Walker, confusion evident in his eyes.

"Is this some sort of joke?" George asked, unable to mask his disbelief.

"Far from it," the officer replied, his tone sombre. "It would seem that Miss Harper might not be as innocent as she appears."

As George continued to examine the files, his initial shock slowly gave way to suspicion. Something didn't sit right with him about this sudden revelation. He glanced up at the officer and mustered his courage to challenge the perceived truth.

"Officer Walker, while I appreciate your diligence, I cannot help but feel that this is yet another attempt to lead us astray. Jessie is a woman of integrity, and I am confident that she is not involved in this crime. If you don't accept my word, I suggest you speak to Detective Sergeant Bill Roberts. "

"Who?" The officer blurted out but then frowned and nodded, understanding George's loyalty to his friend. "Very well, Mr. Jenkins. But I had to bring this to your attention. It is my duty, after all."

"Of course," George conceded, as he handed the folder back to the officer. "But let us not allow these distractions to cloud our judgment or deter us from seeking the truth."

As the day wore on, George couldn't shake the feeling of unease that had settled over him. He noticed that the once-friendly community seemed to be splintering, as gossip and doubt began to spread like wildfire. It was becoming abundantly clear that Jessie and he were now viewed with suspicion by many of their fellow townsfolk.

As they walked through the Old Swan village together later that day, George couldn't help but notice the averted gazes and whispers that trailed in their wake. It was disheartening to see how quickly trust could dissolve into uncertainty and fear.

"Jessie," he began cautiously, "have you noticed how people are treating us?"

"Indeed," she replied with a sigh. "It seems our investigation has stirred up quite the hornet's nest. I'm afraid we're becoming rather unpopular."

"Unfortunate, yes," George agreed. "But let us not allow this to deter us from our purpose. We must remain steadfast in our pursuit of the truth, no matter the consequences."

"Quite right," Jessie declared, a determined glint in her eye. "We shall not waver, nor allow ourselves to be swayed by these attempts to undermine our resolve."

Together, they steeled themselves against the rising tide of mistrust and misdirection, vowing to unearth the truth that lay buried beneath the web of deceit that had ensnared their once-peaceful community. And though the path ahead was shrouded in uncertainty, they knew they could rely on one another to navigate the treacherous journey that awaited them.

GEORGE ACCOMPANIED Jessie to the home of Beatrice Smythe who appeared surprised to see them but was cordial.

"Beatrice, I must speak with you once more" Jessie declared as she entered the sitting room where Beatrice Smythe, the enigmatic psychic, sat immersed in a thick volume. Her silken scarf, adorned with a myriad of shimmering beads, rustled softly as she looked up, her piercing blue eyes narrowing slightly.

"Ah, Miss Harper," Beatrice said coolly, closing the book and setting it aside. "To what do I owe this unexpected intrusion?"

"Forgive me for being so abrupt," Jessie replied, her tone firm yet polite. "But there is a matter of great import that I must discuss with you. It concerns the evidence that was found near the library."

"Go on," Beatrice urged, her expression inscrutable.

"I think someone has planted this evidence to implicate you in the crime," Jessie stated, watching Beatrice closely for any sign of unease. "I believe it is too convenient, and I cannot help but wonder if you are being framed."

"Indeed?" Beatrice raised a slender eyebrow. "And why would someone wish to frame me, pray tell?"

"Perhaps to divert attention from their own misdeeds," Jessie suggested, her gaze unwavering. "Or possibly to sow discord among the community."

"Your suspicions are unfounded, Miss Harper," Beatrice retorted icily. "I have no involvement in this sordid affair, nor do I know who might be attempting to incriminate me. However, I suggest you tread carefully. There are forces at work here beyond your comprehension."

"Is that a threat, Madam Smythe?" Jessie queried, her voice edged with steel.

"Merely a warning," Beatrice replied enigmatically, her lips curling into a faint, thin, mysterious smirk.

As their conversation grew more intense, Jessie felt an uneasy sensation creeping over her like a cold mist. She suddenly realized that Khan had been absent from her side throughout the entire exchange.

"Khan!" she called out nervously, her eyes darting around the room in search of the elusive feline. "Where are you?"

"Looking for your feline companion?" Beatrice asked, an ominous note creeping into her voice. "Perhaps he has decided to distance himself from this sordid business."

"Khan would never abandon me," Jessie replied sharply, her heart beginning to race with concern for her friend. She hastily excused herself from Beatrice's presence and, with George beside her, launched into a frantic pursuit of the missing cat.

"Jessie, over here!" George called out as he spotted a trail of disturbed dust leading towards a heavy wooden door. They threw it open, revealing a dark, dank cellar shrouded in shadows.

"Khan!" Jessie cried out in relief as they found him trapped beneath a pile of old crates, his green eyes glittering with indignation.

"Thank heavens we found you," Jessie murmured, gently extricating him from his confinement. "Are you hurt?"

"Only my dignity, I assure you," Khan replied gruffly, his tail flicking irritably. "I was investigating a strange scent when someone – or something – toppled those crates upon me. It seems our adversary is determined to silence even the most discreet of investigators."

"Indeed," Jessie murmured thoughtfully, cradling Khan in her arms as they emerged from the gloomy depths of the cellar. "We must be more vigilant than ever, for it is clear that the killer is growing desperate – and there is no telling what desperate people might do."

THE TOWN HALL WAS ALIVE with the murmur of anxious voices, as Bill Roberts stepped onto the platform. Jessie, George, and Khan - invisible to all but Jessie - stood near the back of the crowded room, their expressions tense. Bill cleared his throat and raised his hands for silence.

"Good evening, ladies and gentlemen," he began, his voice echoing throughout the hall. "I have called this meeting to address the recent events that have shaken our community. I stand before you not only as a police officer but also as a concerned citizen."

"Jessie Harper and George Jenkins are two individuals who have dedicated themselves to solving the mysterious death of Rosie O'Grady. Yet some of you have accused them of being involved in the crime itself." Bill's gaze swept across the sea of faces, holding each one accountable. "I am here to tell you that these accusations are unfounded. Jessie and George are committed to finding the truth, and I ask you to support them in their efforts."

A ripple of whispers spread through the crowd, and though some nodded in agreement, others exchanged wary glances. Jessie felt her cheeks flush with indignation, but she held her tongue, her fingers tightening around Khan's velvety fur.

Bill continued, "I must also tell you someone or some organization is going to great lengths to discredit these two, Jessie in particular. It seems a man impersonating a police constable handed over false documents purporting to prove Jessie Haper was part of the syndicate behind the death of Rosie and the art heist. This is not only untrue but despicable."

"Thank you, Detective Sergeant Roberts," she whispered to herself, her gaze locked on the man who had become both mentor and friend. "We won't let you down."

Chapter 18

AFTER THE TOWN HALL meeting ended, Jessie, George, and Khan retreated to the privacy of their office, where they could discuss their next move without fear of eavesdropping ears. Jessie paced the floor, her brow furrowed in thought.

"Bill is right," she declared, coming to a halt beside George's desk. "Someone is possibly trying to frame Beatrice, and Albert Humphries, perhaps even me, to divert our attention from the real killer."

"Quite right, Jessie," George agreed, his hands folded on the desk before him. "We mustn't allow ourselves to be led astray by these red herrings."

"Indeed," Khan chimed in, his tail twitching with agitation. "Our adversary has proven themselves cunning and resourceful, but they have not yet defeated us."

"Then we must consider a possibility that we have not yet entertained," Jessie said, her green eyes alight with determination. "The killer may well be someone we have not previously considered."

"By Jove, Jessie, you may be onto something!" George exclaimed, sitting up straighter in his chair. "A person who has thus far remained hidden in plain sight, waiting for the right moment to strike."

"Let us re-examine our list of suspects and see if there is anyone we've overlooked," Jessie suggested, retrieving a sheaf of papers from a nearby shelf.

As they pored over their notes late into the night, Jessie could feel the weight of suspicion and fear hanging heavy upon the community. But she refused to be deterred; she would not rest until the true culprit was brought to justice. With Khan by her side and George's unwavering support, Jessie Harper knew that the truth would prevail - it was only a matter of time.

"Only one way to find out," George replied, his voice steady. "Let us question Albert Humphries in more detail about his past and see if there is any connection between him and this box and its contents you found outside the library."

WITH THAT DECIDED, the trio made their way to the residence of Albert Humphries. The man himself opened the door with an air of wary curiosity, his eyes darting back and forth between Jessie and George.

"Miss Harper, Mr. Jenkins," he greeted them, his voice hesitant. "What brings you to my humble abode?"

"Mr. Humphries," Jessie began, holding up the antique silver mirror. "We found this and wondered if you might recognize it."

"Ah," Albert's face paled, his hands trembling as he took in the sight of the mirror. "You see, I was accused once before, in a similar case. But I assure you, I was innocent then and I am innocent now."

"Tell us more about that accusation, Mr. Humphries," George urged, his tone firm yet sympathetic.

"Very well," Albert sighed, his shoulders slumping. "It happened years ago, in another town. A woman was murdered, and they found a silver mirror like this one near her body. They accused me, but there was never enough evidence to convict me. I've tried to put that dark chapter behind me, but it seems it has followed me here."

"Have you received any threats?" Jessie asked, her voice laced with concern.

"Indeed, I have," Albert admitted, casting a furtive glance over his shoulder. "Anonymous letters warning me to leave town or suffer the consequences. I fear someone is attempting to frame me for this ghastly crime, just as they did before."

"Rest assured, Mr. Humphries," Jessie said firmly, her eyes locking onto his. "We will get to the bottom of this and unmask the true villain. Nothing will deter us from our pursuit of justice."

"Thank you, Miss Jessie," Albert replied, his voice wavering with gratitude. "I only hope that the truth comes to light before it's too late."

With renewed vigour, Jessie, George, and Khan left Albert's residence, their minds racing with the implications of their discovery. Each clue brought them closer to the truth, even as an unseen hand sought to steer them off course. But Jessie Harper would not be so easily led astray, and she vowed to herself that the killer's identity would be unveiled, no matter the cost.

"Next stop, Geraldine Finch," Jessie announced as they strode away from Albert Humphries' residence. "She's our best bet to find any information on this peculiar mirror." George nodded his agreement, and Khan flicked his tail in anticipation.

UPON ARRIVING AT GERALDINE'S home, they found the elderly woman seated in an armchair, surrounded by stacks of dusty books. She adjusted her spectacles and peered at them curiously.

"Miss Finch," Jessie began, "we were hoping you might help us identify this object we recently found." She extended her hand, revealing the antique mirror.

Geraldine gasped softly and paled at the sight of the trinket. She reached for it hesitantly, her hands trembling ever so slightly.

"Wherever did you find this?" she whispered, her voice strained.

"No matter but we do think it may be connected to Rosie's murder," George explained, watching her closely. "Do you recognize it?"

"Perhaps... but I cannot say for certain," Geraldine replied evasively, her eyes darting between the mirror and her visitors. "I must consult my books."

"Please do, Miss Finch," Jessie urged, sensing that Geraldine was withholding something. "We need all the information we can get to solve this case and bring the guilty party to justice."

As Geraldine shuffled through her extensive collection, Jessie exchanged a knowing glance with George. They both understood that their presence was putting pressure on the elderly woman, but they also knew that time was of the essence.

"Ah, here it is," Geraldine declared moments later, pulling out a thick, leather-bound volume. She carefully opened it to a page marked by a frayed ribbon. "The item bears a striking resemblance to one that belonged to a local family generations ago..."

"Which family?" George probed, leaning forward with interest.

"Does it matter?" Geraldine snapped, suddenly defensive. "It's ancient history."

"Miss Finch," Jessie interjected calmly, "we believe this mirror may be the key to solving the murder. We must know everything about it and its possible connection to the case."

Geraldine sighed heavily, her shoulders slumping in resignation. "It belonged to the Worthingtons, a once-prominent family who met a tragic end. It is said that they were cursed by the very item you hold in your hand."

"Curse or not," George mused, "this seems like an intentional attempt to direct our investigation elsewhere."

"Indeed," Jessie agreed, her brow furrowing in determination. "We cannot allow ourselves to be manipulated any longer. We must uncover the truth, no matter the obstacles placed before us."

"Thank you for your help, Miss Finch," Jessie added, pocketing the mirror. "Your expertise has been invaluable."

"Good luck with your investigation," Geraldine murmured as they took their leave. "I fear you'll need it."

Chapter 19

MEANWHILE BACK AT THE office, and undeterred by the mounting suspicion from some in the community, Jessie, George, and Khan redoubled their efforts, combing through every shred of evidence and re-examining each lead. They knew that the real killer was still at large, lurking in the shadows, and they would stop at nothing to bring them to justice.

"Stay vigilant," Jessie warned her companions as they ventured deeper into their investigation. "We can trust no one but each other. The killer may be closer than we think."

"Jessie," George began, his voice hushed, "do you have any idea who might be behind this elaborate deception?"

Jessie shook her head, her auburn hair brushing against her collar. "I wish I did, but the more we uncover, the more tangled this web becomes. It's as if the killer is always one step ahead of us."

"Indeed," Khan chimed in, his green eyes glittering with determination. "But we cannot afford to let our guard down. The very lives of those around us depend on our success in unmasking the culprit."

As they continued their pursuit, Jessie could feel the pressure mounting. Each day brought new challenges and new attempts to mislead them, but she remained steadfast in her resolve.

"Remember," she cautioned, "trust no one but each other. The killer may wear a familiar face, but their heart is blackened by deceit and malice."

"Right you are, Jessie," George concurred, his jaw set in a grim line. "We must rely on our wits and intuition to guide us through this treacherous landscape."

"Meow," Khan agreed sagely, flicking his tail in silent assent.

The trio delved deeper into the case, their collective senses sharpened by the ever-present threat lurking just out of sight. They pored over dusty volumes in the library, interrogated reluctant witnesses, and retraced their steps through the twisted streets of the town.

"George," Jessie mused aloud, "have you noticed how the evidence seems to lead us in circles? It's as if someone is intentionally trying to confound us."

"Curiouser and curiouser," he replied, rubbing his chin thoughtfully. "It seems that as we close in on the truth, the obstacles multiply tenfold."

"Let us not despair," Khan counselled, his fur bristling with anticipation. "Our adversary's desperation only serves to confirm that we are on the right track."

"Indeed," Jessie acknowledged, her eyes flashing with renewed determination. "We must press on and trust in our instincts. The truth will out, no matter how well-hidden it may be."

The mystery deepened with every passing day, the shadows lengthening over the once-idyllic hamlet of Old Swan, now a Liverpool suburb that thinks of itself as a village. But Jessie, George, and Khan refused to waver in their pursuit of justice, resolute in their quest to unmask the villain who had cast a pall over their lives.

Steeling themselves against the increasing pressure from the killer, they vowed to remain vigilant, trusting only in each other as they navigated the perilous path before them.

"Khan," Jessie whispered one evening as they prepared for another round of inquiries, "I cannot shake the feeling that we are being watched. Do you sense anything amiss?"

"Meow," he replied cryptically, his eyes narrowing with suspicion. "I too have felt a malevolent presence lurking nearby. We must tread carefully, for the killer is growing bolder by the hour."

"Let us proceed with caution," George advised, his voice steady despite the mounting tension. "The game is afoot, my friends, and it falls to us to bring this dark chapter to a close."

Armed with their unwavering determination and keen intellects, Jessie, George, and Khan plunged headlong into the fray, ready to face whatever dangers lay in wait. As the investigation continued, our sleuths, human and feline, could not help but be drawn further into the intricate web of intrigue, eager to discover the identity of the elusive killer who threatened to destroy their world.

Chapter 20

JESSIE HARPER'S NIMBLE fingers worked their way through the old archives at Liverpool Central Library. The scent of musty paper and worn leather filled her nostrils as she searched for any information that could connect Rosie O'Grady to the infamous art heist that had plagued the city decades ago.

"Ah, here we are," Jessie whispered, her excitement barely contained, as her eyes scanned an aged newspaper article detailing the theft of a renowned artist's masterpiece. She couldn't believe her luck when, in a small follow-up piece, she found Rosie's name mentioned as a person of interest in the case. It seemed the police hadn't been able to gather enough evidence against her, but this raised even more questions about Rosie's mysterious past, including why Jessie had never known her birth mother.

"George, you need to see this," Jessie called out, clutching the newspaper cutting tightly. George ambled over, his cane clicking rhythmically against the library floor.

"Good heavens, Jessie! This is quite a find," George exclaimed after studying the article. "We have a new mystery on our hands, it seems."

"Indeed," Jessie agreed, determination settling into her features. "I think it's time we dig deeper into this world of art and uncover the truth behind Rosie's involvement."

"Agreed," George nodded, his face alight with enthusiasm. "Let's start by paying a visit to Inspector Hopkinson, who was in charge of the case back then."

Together, they made their way to the suburban Allerton home of retired Inspector Hopkinson, who had overseen the art heist investigation. Upon arriving, they found the elderly man tending to his roses, pruning shears in hand.

"Inspector," Jessie began, her voice firm but respectful. "We're here to discuss the art theft you investigated years ago. We believe it may be connected to a recent murder."

"Ah, yes," Hopkinson sighed, setting down his shears and wiping his brow with a worn handkerchief. "That case has haunted me for years. The stolen painting was said to have paranormal properties, you know. Many believed it brought misfortune to its owners."

"Paranormal properties?" Jessie questioned, a chill running down her spine.

"Indeed," Hopkinson nodded solemnly. "It was said that the painting held a dark power, one that could bring ruin upon those who possessed it."

"Could such a thing truly be real?" George mused aloud, his scepticism apparent in the arch of his eyebrow. Jessie, however, felt a shiver of fear. The world of the paranormal was all too familiar to her, and she knew better than to dismiss such possibilities outright.

"Whether or not the painting's abilities are genuine, there can be no doubt that someone believed them to be," Jessie said, her voice steady despite the quickening of her pulse. "And that belief could be enough to drive someone to commit murder."

"Very true," Hopkinson agreed, his gaze distant as he recalled the details of the long-unsolved case. "Perhaps it is time for this mystery to finally be laid to rest."

"Indeed," Jessie echoed, her resolve hardening like steel within her. "For Rosie's sake, we will find the truth – no matter the cost."

"Curiouser and curiouser," Jessie murmured, her mind racing with possibilities. She glanced at Khan, her enigmatic black cat, who sat silently in the corner, his green eyes narrowed in concentration. Jessie had to remind herself that she was the only human present who could see Khan.

"Thank you, Inspector Hopkinson," Jessie said politely as they took their leave. "Your insights have been invaluable."

"Always happy to help, Miss Harper," Hopkinson replied, a hint of nostalgia in his voice, "You should check out the seedy art district, you know."

"We will, thank you once more," Jessie said.

AS JESSIE AND GEORGE delved deeper into the shadier corners of the city's art scene, they were met with resistance and even threats from those who wished to keep the painting's location a secret. Their footsteps echoed through dimly lit alleyways, leading them further into the labyrinthine underbelly of the city's underworld inhabited by criminals and ne'er-do-wells of all shapes and sizes. The air thickened with an unspoken tension as they approached the clandestine network of artists and collectors who guarded the painting's elusive whereabouts.

"Go! Get gone!" They heard faint but audible whispers drifting through the shadows, warning of the dangers they were about to face. Strangers, whose mouths stayed shut, but with unfriendly glances, loaded with disdain, followed their every move, like sentinels protecting a hidden treasure. Each encounter dripped with veiled hostility, hinting at the desperation of those who sought to preserve the painting's secrecy.

But it wasn't just icy stares and hushed conversations that Jessie and George encountered. Figments of the imagination flapped in front of them. But were they? Or were they real? The invisible hands of coercion crept closer, tightening their grip with each step forward. They received cryptic messages, laced with ominous undertones, threatening dire consequences should they persist in their quest for the painting's truth.

Undeterred, Jessie and George pressed on, unwavering in their determination. With every obstacle they faced, their resolve grew stronger, their curiosity burning like a smouldering flame. It was a dangerous dance, entangling them in a web of secrets and hidden intentions, where revealing the painting's location could shatter the delicate balance of power.

In this treacherous journey into the heart of the city's underworld, Jessie and George were forced to rely on their instincts and cunning. They uncovered fragments of truth, piecing together a puzzle that had been meticulously shattered, while weaving through a tapestry of whispers, half-truths, and veiled threats.

The more resistance they encountered, the more they understood the significance of what they sought. The painting held secrets that transcended its physical form, secrets capable of shaking the foundation of the art world. With every breathless confrontation and clandestine encounter, Jessie and George delved deeper into the murky realm of the city's artistic enigma, unravelling a tapestry of danger and intrigue that threatened to consume them.

"Jessie, we must tread carefully," George warned. "It seems we're getting closer to something big. And what is more, something we truly do not comprehend."

"Indeed," Jessie agreed, her brows furrowed in thought. "But we can't back down now. There's too much at stake."

Khan, ever vigilant, used his invisibility to snoop around the art shops and underground markets, overhearing conversations about the stolen painting's recent sightings. He informed Jessie of a potential lead that could bring them closer to the truth. "He will come to you after you take your seats at that café over there."

"Good work, Khan," Jessie praised, her eyes gleaming with determination. "Now, let's follow this lead and see where it takes us."

Little did they know, as they pursued the trail of the stolen masterpiece, just how intertwined the theft was with the dark secrets of Rosie's past and the dangerous criminal syndicate that lurked in the shadows.

Chapter 21

JESSIE'S FINGERS DRUMMED on the wooden table, her eyes scanning the room as she and George waited in a dimly lit café. The aroma of freshly ground coffee mingled with the faint scent of cigars, while soft murmurs of conversation filled the air. Time seemed to stretch interminably as they awaited their informant.

"Here he comes," George whispered, nodding towards a shuffling shadowy figure who approached their table, his shuffling revealing his hesitancy.

"Evening," the man said, taking a seat across from them. His hands trembled slightly as he wiped beads of sweat from his brow. "I'm told you're interested in a certain painting."

"Indeed," Jessie replied, leaning forward. "We believe it may be connected to a murder investigation we're conducting."

"Ah, I see." The man glanced around nervously before continuing. "Well, I've heard whispers. It's been seen recently, in the possession of a rather... unsavoury character."

"Can you give us a name?" George asked, his voice firm yet non-threatening.

"Sorry, I don't know his name, but I can tell you where he operates," the man said, swallowing hard. "There's a half-empty warehouse down by the docks. You might find what you're looking for there."

"Thank you," Jessie said, her gaze steady on the informant. "We appreciate your help."

"Of course, Miss," he replied, managing a weak smile. "Just be careful. There are dangerous people involved in this."

"Understood," Jessie replied. As the man left, she turned to George, her mind racing. "George, if this lead takes us to the painting, it could finally reveal the connection between Rosie and the theft all those years ago."

"True," George agreed, his jaw set with determination. "But let's not forget the danger we're walking into. These criminals aren't to be trifled with."

"Agreed," Jessie said, her heart heavy with the weight of their mission. "But we must see this through, for Rosie and her family's sake."

"Absolutely," George responded, his voice resolute.

As they left the café, Jessie couldn't help but feel a sense of foreboding, knowing that each step brought them closer to the heart of a deadly conspiracy. But with George at her side and Khan's supernatural abilities aiding them, she was determined to uncover the truth and bring justice to those who deserved it.

"Are you all right to walk over to the warehouses, George? I see you are struggling a bit."

"I'm fine, Jessie, but thanks for asking."

"Khan," Jessie whispered, her voice barely audible as she leaned close to the sleek black cat. "I need you to do some reconnaissance for us. We'll be visiting several warehouses. I believe there we will find some dishonest art dealers and possibly their bodyguards."

"Understood," Khan replied, his vibrant green eyes betraying no emotion.

"Remember, keep an eye out for any signs of the stolen painting or mentions of Rosie," Jessie instructed, though she knew Khan was already aware of their mission. With a flick of his tail, he vanished from sight, his presence only detectable by the faint whisper of his voice in Jessie's ear.

"Of course," came the disembodied reply, reassuring Jessie of the feline's unwavering loyalty.

Jessie turned to George, who stood nearby, his cane tapping rhythmically against the cobblestone street. "Ready?" she asked, her expression taut with apprehension.

"Always," George responded, his own face reflecting a determination that matched Jessie's.

Together, they made their way towards the docks through the narrow alleyways and bustling streets of Liverpool, stopping at various warehouses seemingly used by art dealers and galleries. They encountered an array of intriguing characters, each one more resistant to their inquiries than the last. Frustration gnawed at Jessie as they left yet another uncooperative establishment, the ponderous door slamming shut behind them like a resounding gavel.

"Jessie," Khan's faint voice whispered in her ear, making her stiffen. "I've overheard something interesting at a shop two streets over. I believe it may be a lead worth following."

"Excellent work, Khan," Jessie murmured, her spirits lifting at the prospect of progress. She relayed the information to George, and they quickened their pace, eager to uncover the secrets that had eluded them thus far.

As they neared the location described by Khan, Jessie felt a prickling sensation at the back of her neck. She couldn't shake the feeling that they were being watched, the sensation akin to a thousand tiny needles piercing her skin. "George," she whispered, her voice barely audible above the cacophony of dockland and city noises. "We must tread carefully. I believe we're being followed."

"Indeed," George agreed, his eyes darting over the surrounding crowd, searching for any sign of a potential threat. "We cannot afford to let our guard down."

"Let's proceed with caution," Jessie added, her resolve unwavering despite the lingering sense of unease.

There it was. Khan was pointing at a shop forming part of a partly occupied six-storey warehouse. Entering the dimly lit shop, George and

Jessie found themselves surrounded by an eclectic array of artwork, each piece more mysterious and intriguing than the last. A man behind the counter eyed them suspiciously, his fingers drumming an impatient rhythm on the polished wood.

"Can I help you?" he asked, his tone clipped and unfriendly.

"Perhaps," Jessie replied, her gaze never leaving the man's face. "We're looking for a painting that has long been thought lost. It has certain...unique properties."

"Ah, yes," the man responded, a sly grin spreading across his face. "I know of such a painting. But it comes with quite the price – one you may not be prepared to pay."

"Try us," George interjected, bristling at the man's insinuation.

"Very well," the man said, leaning in conspiratorially. "But remember, you asked for this."

As Jessie listened intently to the information being divulged, she couldn't help but feel that this revelation was only the beginning, and that danger lurked just around the corner. With every new detail gleaned, the stakes grew higher, the truth drawing closer within reach. Yet, despite the risks, Jessie remained steadfast in her pursuit of justice. For Rosie, for her family, and for herself – there was simply no turning back.

Chapter 22

JESSIE AND GEORGE KNEW intuitively they had to discover more facts about the theft of the artwork so this time with George in tow, Jessie returned to the archives in the library.

"Thank you," Jessie murmured, her eyes scanning the article quickly as she realised this information was what she was looking for. The theft had involved a masterpiece by a renowned artist, a painting as enigmatic as it was beautiful – but the case remained cold, even after all these years.

As Jessie continued to peruse the archives, she noticed another small article tucked away in the corner, barely visible. Curiosity piqued, she squinted at the faded words, which seemed to leap off the page and grab her by the throat.

"Rosie O'Grady" – the name was unmistakable, printed there in black and white for the world to see. According to this follow-up piece, Rosie had been a person of interest in the heist, but the police hadn't found enough evidence to make a case against her. This revelation sent a shiver down Jessie's spine – what did it mean for her connection to Rosie? Why had she never known that Rosie was her birth mother?

"Rosie," Jessie whispered to herself, feeling as though the very walls of the library were closing in on her. "What have you gotten yourself into?"

Her mind raced with questions, each one more pressing than the last. The art heist, Rosie's mysterious past, the tenuous thread that seemed to connect them both – it was a puzzle whose pieces refused to fit together. Then there was the connection to the occult and a secret society. And... for goodness' sake... where did Reverend Bennett, Humphries, Smythe, and Finch fit into the jigsaw?

"Could this be the key?" Jessie pondered, running her fingertips over the words on the page. "Is this the secret that's been hidden from me all these years?"

Only one thing was certain: Jessie Harper would not rest until she had uncovered the truth. No matter how deep she had to dig or how many stones she had to overturn, she would find the answers she sought. For herself, for Rosie, and for the truth that had eluded them both for far too long.

JESSIE COULD BARELY contain herself as she hurried to the office, clutching the newspaper clipping tightly in her hand. The scent of leather and old paper wafted through the air as she pushed open the door, finding George immersed in a stack of documents.

"George!" Jessie exclaimed, her eyes sparkling with excitement. "You won't believe what I've found!"

"Jessie, my dear," George replied, peering up from his work with a mixture of curiosity and amusement. "Do tell."

"Look at this." She handed him the aged piece of newsprint, watching as his eyes scanned the text. "It's about an art heist that happened decades ago. And Rosie's name is mentioned in connection with it."

"Good heavens," George murmured, his brow furrowing in concern. "How did we not come across this earlier? I am not going to ask how you now suddenly come to be in possession of it."

"No. Don't. Let's just say it's borrowed and leave it at that. As for your other point, it was hidden in the archives like a needle in a haystack," she replied, her mind racing with possibilities. "But now that we have it, we need to delve deeper into this mystery. It could be the key to understanding why Rosie was murdered."

"Indeed," George agreed, rising from his chair with renewed vigour. "Let us not waste any more time. We must follow this lead."

Chapter 23

ONCE MORE, JESSIE AND George found themselves navigating the streets of Liverpool's art district, where reputable galleries stood alongside disreputable establishments. Reputable people stood cheek by jowl with ruffians, and they all dressed the same and talked the same language – money. The air was thick with tension, as if even the walls knew the grim secrets lurking within these storied buildings.

"Are you sure this is the best way to find information about the stolen painting?" George asked Jessie, his gaze flitting nervously between the dark alleys and the imposing facades of the art shops.

"Inspector Hopkinson said that the painting might have passed through the hands of some rather unsavoury characters," Jessie replied, her voice firm but quiet as she eyed each shop they passed. "So, we must explore every avenue."

"Quite right," George murmured, straightening his spine as they approached a particularly seedy-looking establishment. "We'll leave no stone unturned."

As they stepped inside one of the shops which seemed to double up as an unlicensed drinking parlour, Jessie felt an uncomfortable shiver crawl up her spine at the sight of the shadowy figures that filled the room. A hush fell over the crowd, as if their presence had breached some unspoken code among the denizens of this underworld.

"May I help you?" a greasy-haired man inquired, his eyes narrowing suspiciously as he scrutinized their faces.

"We're looking for information on a certain painting," George began, only to be cut off by a low growl from one of the patrons.

"Nobody here knows nothing about nothing, never mind a painting," the man warned, his voice tinged with menace.

"Of course not," Jessie interjected smoothly, her heart pounding in her chest as she tried to maintain her composure. "We were just hoping for some guidance on where such a piece might be found."

"Look elsewhere," the greasy-haired man advised coldly before turning away, effectively dismissing them.

"Charming fellow," George muttered under his breath as they hastily exited the shop.

"Indeed," Jessie agreed, clenching her fists in frustration. "But we can't be deterred by their resistance – it only proves that we're on the right track."

"Agreed," George said, his determination matching hers. "So, where to next?"

"Let's try a different tactic," Jessie suggested, looking around for any sign of Khan. She spotted him lurking nearby and beckoned him over. "Khan, can you use your invisibility to snoop around these shops? We need any information about the stolen painting's recent sightings."

"Of course," the cat replied in a hushed tone, his green eyes gleaming with excitement. "I'll be back shortly."

As they waited for Khan's return, George and Jessie continued their search for information, facing more resistance and veiled threats along the way. Their resolve never wavered, each encounter making them more certain that the truth was close at hand.

Finally, Khan reappeared, his eyes wide with urgency. "Jessie, I've found something," he whispered, his tail flicking back and forth as he relayed what he'd overheard. "There's a potential lead - a man who was boasting about acquiring a painting with a dark history."

"Where can we find this man?" Jessie asked, her pulse quickening as she sensed the importance of Khan's discovery.

"Follow me," Khan instructed, leading them through the streets with purpose. As they walked, Jessie couldn't help but feel that they were on the precipice of uncovering a vital piece of the puzzle – one that would bring them closer to unravelling the truth behind Rosie's murder and the stolen painting's mysterious past.

Khan, that enigmatic feline with emerald eyes, led Jessie and George through a web of narrow alleys and hidden passages until they reached a nondescript door, partially concealed behind a stack of wooden crates. The cat paused, his ears twitching as he scanned the area for signs of danger.

"Is this the place?" Jessie inquired, her auburn hair catching the dim light from a nearby streetlamp. Her keen librarian's eye took note of the door's worn appearance, the peeling paint and rusty hinges suggesting it had seen better days.

"Indeed," Khan confirmed, his voice barely a whisper. "The man you seek is inside."

Jessie exchanged a resolute glance with George before rapping firmly on the door. A tense silence settled over them as they waited, the seconds stretching into an eternity before the door creaked open to reveal a small, balding man with beady eyes and a slight hunch.

"Can I help you?" he asked cautiously, his gaze darting between the two strangers and the black cat at their feet.

"Word has it that you've recently acquired a painting with a rather... dark history," Jessie began, choosing her words carefully. "We'd like to have a word with you about it."

The man hesitated and then, with a glance at Khan, ushered them inside. As they entered the cramped space, Jessie couldn't help but notice its walls lined with various pieces of artwork, some authentic and others clearly counterfeit. George remained silent, his muscular frame tense and watchful as they followed their host.

"Please, have a seat," the man gestured to a threadbare couch, his eyes still fixed warily on Khan. "I don't know what you've heard, and I don't ask questions when it comes to business."

"Then let me be plain," Jessie said, her voice steady and authoritative. "We have reason to believe that the painting in question may be connected to a recent murder."

"Murder?" The man's eyes widened, his voice rising with genuine surprise. "I don't want any part of that!"

"Nor do we," George interjected gruffly. "But we need to know how you came into possession of the painting and who might be looking for it."

The man hesitated, wringing his hands nervously. "I acquired it through... let's call them 'unconventional channels'. There was a rumour that the painting was cursed, but I didn't take it seriously."

"Perhaps you should have," Jessie mused, her thoughts racing as she considered the implications. Could it be possible that the art theft and Rosie's murder were linked? Her heart constricted at the thought of her birth mother, a woman she'd never known, caught up in such a dangerous web.

"Someone is clearly willing to kill to reclaim this painting," George added, his jaw set with determination. "We need to find out who they are before they strike again."

"Alright," the man relented, fear etched onto his face. "There's an underground auction happening tonight. It's invitation-only, and I'd wager that whoever's behind all this will be there."

"Take us to it," Jessie demanded, her resolve hardening. The man nodded reluctantly, clearly realizing that he had little choice but to comply.

As they prepared to leave, Jessie couldn't help but ponder the twisted threads connecting the stolen painting to Rosie's murder. It seemed increasingly likely that a dangerous criminal syndicate was involved, and every step they took brought them closer to unmasking the truth. Tonight, perhaps, they would finally uncover the malevolent force lurking in the shadows and bring justice to Rosie's memory.

Chapter 24

DETECTIVE SERGEANT Bill Roberts had tracked down Joyce and Ellen, Rosie's daughters, and now Jessie invited them to the Dale Steet office to ask them some questions.

Jessie observed the wariness of the sisters, as they sat huddled together on the threadbare sofa. Their eyes darted between her and George, apprehension etched onto their faces.

"Joyce, Ellen," Jessie began, adopting a gentle tone. "We have reason to believe that your mother's murder may be connected to the stolen painting we've been investigating."

Ellen's grip on Joyce's hand tightened noticeably. "What do you mean?" she asked, her voice quivering.

"Did Rosie ever mention anything about a painting or receive any threats before her death?" George inquired, studying the sisters' reactions closely.

After a moment's hesitation, Joyce spoke up. "She received an anonymous letter a few days before...before it happened. It mentioned the stolen painting and warned her that 'the past has a way of catching up.'"

"Did she keep the letter?" Jessie's heart raced at this new piece of information.

"No," Joyce replied regretfully. "She burned it in the fireplace. She didn't want us to worry."

"Was there anything else?" George prodded gently.

"Actually, yes," Ellen interjected, her voice barely audible. "The day before she died, she met with a mysterious man at the warehouse."

"How do you know this?" Jessie said.

"We went with her because she asked us. She was scared... like."

"Can you describe him?" Jessie inquired, sensing the importance of this revelation.

"Only that he was tall and wore a dark coat," Ellen offered, her eyes downcast. "We didn't see his face."

"Thank you, both of you," Jessie said softly, feeling a swell of empathy for the burden they bore. As the sisters clasped each other's hands, Jessie shared a glance with George, her thoughts racing.

"George," she whispered, pulling him aside. "It's clear the same syndicate that orchestrated the art theft is after Joyce and Ellen as well. They must believe the sisters have information about the painting's location."

"Agreed," George nodded grimly. "We need to ensure their safety while we continue our investigation."

Jessie's determination flared, her resolve hardening as she considered the implications of this new information. The stakes were higher now, and the threat more menacing than ever before. But she would not waver; for Rosie and her daughters, Jessie would unearth the truth, no matter where it led or who stood in her way.

"Let's get them to a secure location," Jessie decided, a steely glint in her eyes. "Then we'll track down this syndicate and put an end to their reign of terror once and for all."

"HERE'S YOUR TEA, JESSIE," George said, handing her a steaming cup as they sat in the corner of a small café. Jessie took a grateful sip, the warmth momentarily steadying her nerves.

"Thank you, George," she murmured, watching as the pedestrian traffic outside bustled along the street. "We need to stay vigilant. The syndicate knows we're getting closer, and there's no telling what they'll do next."

"Agreed." George's voice was grave as he took a sip of his own tea, his eyes scanning the surroundings attentively. "So, what's our next move?"

Jessie held the cup close, feeling its heat against her fingers as she contemplated their options. A plan formed in her mind, one that would require cunning and courage, but could potentially ensnare the very criminals who had so far eluded them.

"Joyce and Ellen are key," she began, her voice low but firm. "If the syndicate believes they have information about the painting, they'll be relentless in their pursuit. We must turn that to our advantage."

"Use them as bait, you mean?" George asked, his brow furrowing in concern.

"Exactly." Jessie met his gaze, her eyes resolute. "We promise them police protection, of course. But if we can lure the syndicate into revealing themselves, it might be the breakthrough we need."

"High stakes, Jessie," George warned, taking another sip of tea as he mulled over the strategy.

"Indeed, but we've no other choice. Rosie's murder, the stolen painting... these threads are intertwined, and we must unravel them before more lives are lost."

"Very well," George agreed at last, setting down his cup with a decisive clack. "Let's bring our plan to Detective Sergeant Roberts and ensure Joyce and Ellen are protected."

"Thank you, George," Jessie said, a brief smile flickering across her lips before she grew serious once more. "Now, we must be cautious. The syndicate could strike at any moment, and we must be prepared."

"Agreed," George nodded solemnly, his eyes returning to their vigilant watch over the café's patrons.

"Let's finish our tea and get moving," Jessie suggested, feeling an uneasy sense of urgency pressing upon her.

As they drained the last drops from their cups and prepared to leave, Jessie couldn't shake the sensation of being watched. Every rustle of a newspaper, every soft murmur of conversation, seemed to carry an undercurrent of menace that sent shivers down her spine.

"Stay close, George," she whispered as they stepped out into the bustling street. "The game is afoot."

Moments later, a figure emerged from the shadows, following Jessie and George with sinister intent. The mysterious syndicate had made its move, and the harrowing encounter that would follow would raise the stakes of their investigation to unforeseen heights.

"GEORGE," JESSIE HISSED as they crouched behind a stack of wooden crates, "I think we've been made. The syndicate must have caught wind of our plan."

"Damn," George muttered under his breath, scanning the dimly lit alleyway for signs of movement. "We can't let them get away with this."

"Stay low and follow my lead," Jessie whispered, her auburn hair falling across her determined eyes as she gripped the cool metal handle of her small cosh.

They crept through the shadows, hearts pounding in their chests as they edged closer to the building where they believed their pursuer was hiding. A sudden scuffle of footsteps echoed through the night, and Jessie tensed, her fingers curling around the weapon.

"Over there," George murmured, nodding towards a figure slipping out of a side door. "That's one of them."

"Let's go!" Jessie urged, as she burst into action, sprinting after the fleeing figure. Adrenaline coursing through her body, Jessie was oblivious to George's whereabouts. The pursuit led her on a thrilling chase through the narrow streets of Liverpool, dodging carts and pedestrians as she struggled to keep up with the agile criminal.

"Split up! I'll go this way; you head him off!" George shouted, veering down a side street while Jessie continued straight ahead.

Hearing his cry, Jessie turned around just in time to see George had commandeered a bicycle and wasn't far behind. Then he vanished down the side street yelling and whirling his cane above his head.

"Be careful!" Jessie called back, her thoughts racing as she focused on tracking the suspect. She couldn't help but worry about George, knowing all too well how dangerous these criminals could be. What if they both ended up like Rosie?

"Look out!" a shrill cry broke Jessie from her thoughts as she narrowly avoided colliding with a young boy selling newspapers. The close call only fuelled her determination, and she pressed on, her breath coming in ragged gasps as she rounded another corner.

"Got you now," Jessie panted, spotting the suspect trapped at a dead end. Her heart sank as she realized George was nowhere in sight, but she steeled herself, raising her cosh with a steady hand.

"Alright, you," she snarled, "tell me everything you know about the syndicate and the whereabouts of the stolen painting."

"Never," the man spat, defiance burning in his eyes. Suddenly, a heavy blow struck him from behind, sending him crumpling to the ground.

"Nice work, Jessie," George panted, clutching his side and leaning heavily on his cane as he emerged from the shadows, one arm looped around the unconscious criminal's collar.

"George!" Jessie cried in relief, rushing to his side. "I thought I'd lost you."

"Can't get rid of me that easily," he grinned, though his face was pale and damp with sweat. "Now let's get this scoundrel back to the station. He'll lead us to the rest of the syndicate, and we'll finally put an end to this nightmare."

"Agreed," Jessie nodded, her resolve hardened by the night's events. "And together, we'll ensure justice is served for Rosie."

BACK AT THE OFFICE, Jessie studied the photograph of the stolen painting, her brow furrowed with concentration as she tried to discern its mystical properties. The artwork depicted a haunting scene, with a turbulent sea and spectral figures surrounding a solitary lighthouse. The image sent shivers down her spine, and she could not help but feel that it held a terrible power.

"George," Jessie said, not taking her eyes off the photograph, "do you recall anything about this painting having paranormal properties?"

"Only rumours based on what people told us," he replied, rifling through the case files spread out on the table before them. "Some claim it brings misfortune to those who possess it."

"Then we must retrieve it at all costs," she declared, her voice tense with urgency. "I have a terrible feeling that if it remains in the hands of the syndicate, it will only bring more pain and suffering."

"Alright," George agreed, his own expression grave. "We'll focus our efforts on finding the painting, and along the way, perhaps we'll uncover the true connection between Rosie and this enigmatic piece of art."

Jessie's thoughts raced with conjecture, each possibility more troubling than the last. Was Rosie involved in the theft? Did the painting somehow lead to her death? What was the connection to the occult and a secret society, if any? She shook her head, frustrated by the mystery that seemed to grow deeper with each new revelation.

"First thing tomorrow," she said, her tone grim, "we'll question the apprehended syndicate member. Perhaps he can shed some light on the location of the painting and the extent of Rosie's involvement."

"Agreed," George replied, rubbing his temples. "I don't like the idea of using Joyce and Ellen as bait any more than you do, Jessie. But we can't allow the syndicate to continue their reign of terror."

"Let's hope our plan works, George," Jessie murmured, her eyes flicking back to the eerie image of the stolen painting. "For all our sakes."

"Indeed," George sighed, sensing the weight of responsibility pressing down on them both. "We'll need to be cautious, but also determined. Together, we can bring these criminals to justice and protect those closest to Rosie."

"Let's just hope we're not too late," Jessie whispered, her heart aching with the thought of what might happen if they failed.

With renewed determination, Jessie and George gathered their belongings and set off into the night. The stakes were high, but they knew they had no choice but to see this mystery through to its end. They would find the stolen painting, bring the syndicate to justice, and uncover the truth about Rosie's connection to the haunting masterpiece.

For themselves, for Rosie, and for all who may yet suffer at the hands of the nefarious criminal organization, they would fight until the very end.

Chapter 25

THE NEXT DAY, JESSIE and George strolled the short distance between their office and the Hatton Garden police station where Bill Roberts had arranged for a meeting with Harry Bentley, a successor to Inspector Hopkinson, in the stolen artwork department of Liverpool's CID. Mr Bentley was a gracious man and gave the two private detectives free rein in handing over all the old files connected to the art heist.

The duo got to work poring over the reams of paperwork, until the silence was broken. "Jessie, look at this," George said, holding up a crumpled newspaper article. The faded text and tattered edges spoke of the passage of time, much like the crow's feet around his eyes.

"Rosie worked as a cleaner at the gallery when the painting was stolen," he continued. Jessie leaned in to examine the article more closely, her auburn hair brushing against George's shoulder.

"Seems we've found another piece of the puzzle," she mused, her keen eyes scanning the words. Inside her mind, thoughts whirled like a vortex, connecting dots and weaving theories together.

"Let me make some inquiries with Bill and my other old contacts from the force," George suggested, standing up and reaching for his cane. "Perhaps they'll have something useful to share."

"Be careful, George," Jessie warned, concern etching lines on her forehead. "We don't know who we can trust."

"Bill Roberts owes me a favour or two," George replied with a grin. "I trust him."

IT WAS ANOTHER SHORT walk to the art gallery and the conversation continued much in the same vein as that at Hatton Garden: "George, your friend Bill told you to tread carefully," Jessie reminded him as they stood outside the Walker Art Gallery, its imposing neo-classical façade casting a shadow over them. "With a powerful syndicate involved, we need to be cautious."

"Indeed, but we also need answers," George replied, adjusting his hat. "Let's see what we can find out about Rosie's time working here."

Inside the gallery, the staff seemed reluctant to divulge information about Rosie O'Grady, but persistence paid off when an older employee shared some insights about the enigmatic cleaner.

"Always secretive, that one," the employee whispered, casting furtive glances around the room. "Never spoke much about her past, not even to the other cleaners."

"Thank you for your help," Jessie said quietly, her suspicions about Rosie growing stronger with each revelation. She shared a significant look with George, and the two continued to wander around the gallery but in contemplative silence.

The questions never ceased, though. If they weren't in the mind, there was always Khan who some might regard as a conundrum in himself.

"Khan, are you certain someone was following us at the auction?" Jessie asked the talking cat, her eyes wide with concern. The sleek black feline flicked his tail and nodded, his bright green eyes never leaving Jessie's face.

"Be on your guard," Khan warned, his voice soft but insistent. "You are being watched."

"George, we need to prepare for any potential dangers," Jessie said, steeling herself for the challenges ahead. "I won't let anyone hurt those I care about."

"Agreed," George replied, his eyes filled with determination. "I'll arrange for extra security at our office, and you should carry a weapon with you, just in case. That little cosh you carry in your bag isn't good enough, I'm afraid. "

"Let's hope it won't come to that," she murmured, her heart heavy with the weight of their investigation.

"George, look at this painting. Don't you think it looks remarkably like the one that was stolen," Jessie exclaimed, excitement bubbling within her as they examined the artwork. "Could it be a forgery?"

"Quite possibly," he agreed, his brow furrowed in concentration. "We must investigate further."

"Excuse me, what are you doing here?" a stern-faced security guard inquired, interrupting their conversation.

"Merely admiring the art," Jessie replied smoothly, mentally preparing herself for another round of questioning. The guard eyed them suspiciously, but eventually let them go without further incident.

"Jessie, we're getting closer," George whispered as they left the museum. "But with each step, the stakes rise higher."

Chapter 26

GEORGE NOTICED AN ENVELOPE on the tiled vestibule floor, the small area between the outside entrance door and the inner door leading to the stairs. He showed the contents to Jessie before folding the note, replacing it in the envelope and then placing it in his jacket pocket. "Time for that later, let's go and see Bill," George said.

"Bill, we've learned a thing or two about this heist," Jessie confided in Detective Bill Roberts as they huddled together in a dimly lit corner of the pub. The scent of stale tobacco smoke and spilled ale clung to the air, but Jessie paid it no mind, her focus solely on the matter at hand. "The painting at the museum could well be a forgery."

"Indeed?" Bill raised an eyebrow, his interest piqued. "That certainly changes things."

"Moreover," George added, leaning forward, the seriousness of his demeanour apparent, "we believe Rosie may have known something about the missing artwork. It's possible that her knowledge made her a target."

"Blimey," Bill muttered, rubbing his chin thoughtfully. "I can see why you're concerned, then. But I must warn you again, tread carefully. This criminal syndicate isn't one to be trifled with."

"Your warning doesn't fall on deaf ears, Bill," Jessie assured him. "But we can't just sit idly by while justice remains unserved."

"Jessie's right," George chimed in, determination evident in his voice. "We need to follow every lead, no matter the danger."

"Very well," Bill sighed, recognizing the stubborn resolve in their eyes. "Just remember, if you ever need backup, I'm here for you both."

"Thank you, Bill. We appreciate your support," Jessie said gratefully, her heart swelling with appreciation for their friend.

"Speaking of leads," George continued, "we attended an art auction recently, hoping to gain some insight into the local art scene."

"Did you now?" Bill asked, intrigued.

"Indeed. We managed to introduce ourselves to a few key personalities," Jessie shared, recalling the various introductions and pleasantries exchanged during the event.

"However," George interjected, casting a furtive glance around the pub, "we were being watched."

"Watched?" Bill's eyes narrowed with concern. "By whom?"

"Khan spotted a suspicious character shadowing us," Jessie explained, her gut churning with unease at the memory. "It confirms our suspicion that we're being watched."

"Stay vigilant," Bill warned, his voice low and urgent. "And keep me informed of any new developments."

"Of course, Bill," Jessie promised, her mind racing with the implications of their discoveries. "This was left in our office entrance earlier today," she added handing over the note and envelope that George had retrieved from his pocket.

Jessie listened as Bill quietly read the note's contents and studied the detective's face. Her fingers were trembling as she listened to Bill's recital of the words that echoed Bill's earlier warning. She glanced at George, who sat alongside her, his face etched with concern mirroring the look on Bill's face.

"Looks like our watcher's decided to send a message," Bill said quietly in his understated way.

"Indeed," Jessie murmured, feeling the weight of those bold, black letters bearing down upon her. "We must tread carefully."

"Let's not let fear dictate our actions, though," George countered, his jaw clenched in determination. "We're close to uncovering the truth, Jessie. We can't back down now."

"Of course not," Jessie agreed, her resolve steeling within her. "But we must take precautions."

"Agreed," George nodded, his mind already racing with ideas for ensuring their safety. "I'll arrange for additional security at the office and see if any contacts can provide us with some form of protection."

"Thank you, George," Jessie whispered, grateful for his unwavering support.

Chapter 27

JESSIE HARPER STOOD outside the posh entrance of the city's exclusive club, The Velvet Quill, adjusting her fancy new hat. The feathers tickling her cheek were a constant reminder that they were navigating the treacherous waters of Liverpool's social elite to investigate Rosie's murder and the theft of the valuable painting. It was a world she had never been part of, and yet here she was, dressed to the nines, with George Jenkins by her side.

"George, do I really need this hat? I feel like a peacock," Jessie whispered nervously as they approached the door.

"Jessie, just think of it as your disguise. Besides, you look quite fetching," George replied, offering her an encouraging smile.

"Fetching? Really?" Jessie raised an eyebrow as a playful smirk crossed her lips. "I suppose that is better than looking like a feather duster."

"Ah, Jessie, always the wit," George chuckled. "Now, let's focus on the task at hand. We need to find out more about the crime syndicate and connections within these circles."

Khan, their talking-cat companion, materialized beside them, wearing a small bow tie that matched George's. "Don't forget about me. I can be quite charming when I want to be," he said, his voice laced with pride.

"Indeed, Khan," Jessie agreed, trying not to laugh at the sight of the cat in formal attire. "You look very dapper."

Once inside The Velvet Quill, they were met with opulence and extravagance beyond anything Jessie had ever seen. Crystal chandeliers hung from the high ceilings, casting a shimmering light on the well-dressed patrons.

The stylish ballroom buzzed with anticipation as the art auction commenced. Jessie peered through the crowd; her auburn hair pinned up in a sophisticated style. The room was adorned with exquisite pieces that would soon change hands, but Jessie's focus remained on the attendees themselves despite Khan's comical capers.

"Remember," George murmured, leaning close to Jessie as they scanned the room, "we're here to gather information. Let's try to make some connections and keep our ears open."

"Right," she agreed, sipping from a delicate champagne flute, her keen eyes taking in every detail.

As the auctioneer introduced the first painting, Jessie and George began mingling with the high-profile guests. They struck up conversations with prominent collectors and dealers, each exchange offering subtle inquiries into the people and events surrounding the notorious heist.

"Such a marvellous Monet," Jessie remarked to an elegantly dressed woman, seizing the opportunity to direct the conversation towards their investigation. "It reminds me of the piece stolen from the local gallery a few years ago – such a tragic loss for the art community."

"Ah, yes," the woman sighed, adjusting her pearl necklace. "That theft was most unfortunate. I heard whispers of a powerful syndicate being involved, but one can never be sure."

"Indeed," Jessie replied thoughtfully, filing away this valuable insight.

"Jessie, look," George whispered, nodding discreetly at a balding man in an impeccably tailored suit. "That's Mr. Worthington, the renowned appraiser. If anyone knows something about the missing painting, it would be him."

"Good thinking," Jessie said, her mind already formulating an approach. The pair wove their way through the crowd, appearing casual yet purposeful.

Meanwhile, Khan stealthily surveyed the scene, invisible to all but Jessie. The black cat's green eyes narrowed, scrutinizing a shadowy figure lingering near the back of the room – a man who seemed to be watching Jessie and George with far too much interest.

"Jessie," Khan whispered in her ear, his words barely audible above the hum of conversation, "we're being observed. There's someone here who doesn't belong."

"Where?" Jessie asked, her heart skipping a beat as she tried to remain composed.

"By the pillar," Khan replied, flicking his tail in the direction of the suspicious character. "He's been following our movements since we arrived."

"George," Jessie murmured without looking at him, "Khan spotted someone watching us. We need to be cautious."

"Understood," George said, his voice steady but concern evident in his dark eyes. "let's play this safe and heed Bill's warning. Let's go home."

THE NEXT DAY THE OFFICE telephone rang, its shrill tone echoing throughout the office space. Jessie picked up the receiver, her brow furrowing as she listened to the voice on the other end.

"Miss Harper," the anonymous caller rasped, "you and your friend would do well to abandon your little investigation. If you don't, I can assure you that there will be... consequences."

"Who is this?" Jessie demanded, her chest tightening with trepidation.

"You were seen at the auction. Consider this a friendly warning," the voice replied before hanging up, leaving Jessie clutching the phone in stunned silence.

"Jessie, what's wrong?" George asked, noting the unease etched on her face.

"Another anonymous threat," she answered, her voice barely above a whisper. "Someone wants us out of this case, George."

"Damned cowards," George muttered, his jaw clenched in anger. "But we won't let them intimidate us, Jessie. We're close to something big here, I can feel it."

"Indeed," Jessie agreed, determination flaring within her. "But we must take precautions."

"Agreed," George nodded. He considered their options for a moment, then said decisively, "I'll arrange for extra security at the office. And I think it's time you started carrying a weapon, Jessie, just in case."

"Are you sure?" Jessie queried, her fingers tracing the contour of her teacup. "I've never been one for violence."

"Neither have I," George admitted, "but these are dangerous times, my dear. We can't afford to be caught unprepared."

"Very well," Jessie conceded, sensing the wisdom in George's words. "What do you suggest?"

"Perhaps a small revolver, concealed in your bag," he proposed, his eyes scanning their surroundings, ever vigilant. "Small enough not to draw attention, but powerful enough to protect yourself if needed."

"All right," Jessie assented, her heart heavy with the weight of their newfound peril. "I suppose there's no harm in being cautious."

"Exactly," George confirmed, his concern for Jessie's safety evident in his gaze. "We'll continue our investigation, but we must be more vigilant than ever."

"Agreed," Jessie said with steely resolve. She would not allow fear to deter her pursuit of justice, but neither would she underestimate the danger they now faced.

Together, they continued their work, their minds focused on the task at hand while their instincts remained on high alert. For Jessie and George knew that their quest for the truth had taken a treacherous turn, and only their wits, courage, and determination would see them through the shadows that lay ahead.

Chapter 28

"I HAVE NO IDEA WHY I haven't thought of this before but all this talk of powerful crime syndicates made me think hard of my time in CID Admin. If I am right, then the most vicious piece of slime on this earth is behind all of this."

"Who, George?"

"Rupert Thorne. To make matters worse he has corrupt officers on his payroll."

"Telephone Bill, George," Jessie implored. "We need to know if our suspicions have been echoed within the force."

"Very well," he replied, dialling the detective's number.

"GEORGE," DETECTIVE Bill Roberts answered cautiously, his voice tinged with unease. "I've got some news for you. Some of my colleagues... they're acting rather unusually. I can't put my finger on it, but I believe there might be corruption related to the syndicate."

"Bill, that's disconcerting," George murmured, the colour draining from his face. "We'd best watch our backs even more closely now. Is it connected to Thorne?"

"It could be but most bad things are connected to him so I can't be sure. Take care and keep me updated."

"Will do, Bill. Goodbye."

"Goodbye, George."

AS GEORGE HUNG UP THE phone, his brow furrowed with concern. He relayed the conversation to Jessie, who bit her lip, her thoughts racing. "Who can we trust now, George?" she whispered, feeling the walls close in around them.

"Only ourselves, Jessie." His eyes bore into hers, steel sharpening their depths. "And Khan, of course."

"Of course," she murmured, a faint smile flickering across her lips.

"Speaking of trust," George said, his gaze shifting toward the list of names they had gathered at the art auction. "One of these personalities may hold the key to unravelling this web."

"Let's pay him a visit," Jessie decided, her determination flaring to life once more. "Perhaps the truth will spill forth when confronted."

"Very well," George agreed, selecting one of the names. "But we tread lightly, Jessie. Remember what's at stake."

"Understood," she replied, her resolve unwavering.

They arrived at an opulent townhouse, its grandeur belying the potential darkness within. Jessie's heart thundered in her chest, a mix of fear and anticipation coursing through her veins as they approached the door.

"Mr. Worthington," George began once they were face-to-face with the art expert suspect, "we have reason to believe you may know something about the stolen painting and the criminal syndicate behind it."

"Preposterous!" the man scoffed, his eyes narrowing. "You've got the wrong person."

"Have we?" Jessie countered, her gaze unyielding. "Or are you merely hiding your true allegiance?"

"Get out," Mr. Worthington snarled, anger flaring in his eyes. "Before I have you both arrested for harassment."

"Very well," George replied, his voice steady. "But remember, Mr. Worthington, the truth has a habit of coming to light."

As they turned to leave, Jessie caught sight of a figure lurking in the shadows, watching them with keen interest. She met George's eyes, her thoughts screaming a warning she dared not voice aloud. The chase was on.

"GEORGE," SHE WHISPERED, urgency lacing her words. "I think we're being followed again."

"Keep walking," he instructed softly, his hand brushing against her arm in reassurance. "We'll lose him in the crowd."

The streets became a maze, Jessie and George weaving through the throng of people with practiced ease. Behind them, the shadowy figure pursued relentlessly, his footsteps echoing in their ears like the ticking of a clock.

"Split up," George urged, his grip tightening on Jessie's arm for a moment before releasing her. "Meet back at the office."

"Be careful," Jessie breathed, her heart pounding as they parted ways.

"Always," he promised, disappearing into the maze of the city.

Jessie's breath came in short gasps, her chest heaving as she ducked into an alleyway to catch her bearings. The shadowy figure had not relented, staying close on her heels despite her best efforts to evade him. Her heart thudded wildly against her ribcage, threatening to burst free from its confines.

"Khan," she whispered urgently, casting a furtive glance around the dimly lit passage. "Where are you?"

A subtle flicker of movement caught her eye, and Khan materialized before her, green eyes piercing the darkness. "I'm here, Jessie," the cat replied, his voice low and steady. "I've been keeping an eye on our pursuer."

"Any ideas on how to shake him off?" Jessie asked, wincing at the tremor in her voice. She was unaccustomed to feeling so vulnerable, so exposed.

"Follow me," Khan instructed, his sleek form slipping down the alleyway with a grace that belied his size. Jessie trailed behind, her footsteps echoing softly on the cobblestones. Together, they navigated the shadows of the city, Khan guiding Jessie deftly through the network of streets until they reached the safety of their office.

"Thank you, Khan," Jessie breathed, sinking into a chair, her legs suddenly weak. "I don't know what I would have done without you."

"Think nothing of it," the cat replied, settling onto her lap. "We cannot allow ourselves to be deterred by the likes of them."

"Them," Jessie murmured, the word heavy with implications. They were no longer dealing with a simple murder investigation - this was something far more insidious. A powerful, dangerous crime syndicate had their sights set on them, and every step brought them further into the lion's den.

The door to the office creaked open, and George entered, his face a mask of concern. "Jessie, are you all right?" he asked, his eyes scanning her for any sign of injury.

"I'm fine," she replied, forcing a weary smile. "But I think it's time we involved Bill more closely in our investigation. I'm content he is entirely trustworthy."

"Agreed," George said, pulling up a chair close to hers. They recounted their discoveries, the connections they'd made, and their growing suspicions about the criminal syndicate's involvement.

"Bill has already warned us about some unusual behaviour within the police ranks," Jessie reminded him. "We need to tread carefully, George. We can't trust just anyone with this information."

"Indeed," George conceded, his brow furrowed in thought. "But we must do something. We cannot allow Rosie's murder to go unsolved, nor can we let these criminals continue their dark deeds unopposed."

"Then we fight," Jessie declared, determination hardening her features. "For Rosie, for justice, and for everyone who has suffered at the hands of this syndicate."

"Very well," George agreed, a resolute glint in his eyes. "Together, we will bring them to their knees."

And so, the stage was set for a battle of wits and cunning against an enemy they had yet to fully comprehend. But one thing was certain: Jessie and George would not rest until justice prevailed, no matter how high the stakes or how dangerous their path.

Chapter 29

"BILL, WE MUST FIND a way to lure this syndicate out into the open," Jessie declared, her fingers drumming nervously on the table. "We've been dancing at the end of the string for far too long."

"Indeed," George concurred, his eyes sharp as he studied the documents strewn across the surface. "But how do we engage such an elusive enemy without putting ourselves at unnecessary risk?"

"Perhaps," Bill mused, tapping his chin thoughtfully, "we can play a little game of our own. We could leak misinformation about our findings, hoping to confuse them and force their hand."

"An intriguing idea," Jessie admitted, her brow creasing with concentration. "But what sort of misinformation would drive them to action?"

"Something that threatens their operation," Bill suggested. "We could imply that we're close to uncovering the identity of one of their key members or the location of their stolen art cache."

"Risky," George muttered, his gaze flickering between Jessie and Bill. "But it may be our best chance to expose them."

"Then let us set the trap," Jessie agreed, determination resonating in her voice. "For Rosie's sake, we must see this through to the end."

The three spent the following hours devising their plan, each contributing their expertise and weaving a web of deception designed to ensnare their adversaries. As they worked, Jessie couldn't help but feel an undercurrent of fear; she knew the stakes had never been higher, and the slightest misstep could spell disaster.

Finally, their strategy was complete, and the trio sat back, exhaustion etched on their faces. Jessie glanced at George, searching his expression for signs of doubt or hesitation. Instead, she found only steely resolve.

"Are you ready for this, George?" she asked softly, her hand resting on his arm.

"Ready as I'll ever be," he replied, offering her a tight smile. "We've come this far; there's no turning back now."

"Then let us brace ourselves for the storm," Jessie said, her grip tightening on George's arm. She knew they were walking a dangerous path, but she couldn't – wouldn't – allow fear to dictate her actions.

"Here's to justice," George murmured, raising an imaginary glass in toast.

"Justice," Jessie echoed, meeting his gaze with fierce determination. Together, they would see this through to the bitter end, no matter what perils lay ahead.

And as the sun dipped below the horizon, casting long shadows across their office, Jessie and George prepared themselves for the battle that was sure to follow. They were aware of the growing danger, but their pursuit of justice – for Rosie O'Grady and all those who had suffered at the hands of the syndicate – drove them forward, unyielding in their resolve.

For in the dark corners of the city, where criminals lurked and corruption festered, Jessie Harper and George Jenkins were a beacon of hope, a force to be reckoned with – and they would not go quietly into the night.

Chapter 30

TO THE UNINFORMED OBSERVER, the young woman with auburn hair was staring into space idling time away. Appearances can be deceptive.

Jessie Harper leaned against the edge of the wooden desk in the detective agency, her gaze fixed on a yellowed newspaper clipping pinned to the board before her. The headline screamed about the infamous art heist that had taken place five years ago, and right below it was a photograph of Rosie O'Grady, looking as if she'd just stepped out of one of her cleaning clients' luxurious residences. It was an unflattering 'Mrs Mop' type of photograph.

"George," Jessie said, tapping the newspaper with her forefinger, "the more I dig into this, the more I'm convinced Rosie's murder is connected to the art heist. We've stumbled upon something much bigger than we first thought."

George Jenkins limped over to join her. His dark eyes scanned the newspaper article and then flicked down to the photograph of Rosie. He nodded slowly, his cane tapping rhythmically against the worn floorboards.

"Indeed, Jessie, it appears so. And if our suspicions are correct, we're dealing with a far-reaching syndicate that won't hesitate to eliminate us if we get too close."

Jessie pushed a loose strand of auburn hair behind her ear and sighed. "We can't let that stop us, though, can we? We owe it to Rosie to uncover the truth."

"Of course not, but we must proceed cautiously." George straightened up and looked at her intently. "I have an idea. What if we go undercover at that high-profile art auction happening this Friday? If there's a connection between Rosie and the heist, we might find some clues there."

"Capital idea, George! I'm game if you are." Jessie smiled, feeling the familiar thrill of the chase electrify her senses.

THE AUCTION HOUSE WAS buzzing with activity, the air thick with anticipation and intrigue. Jessie and George, on this occasion were clad in inconspicuous clothing, surveyed the room. They noted the suspicious characters milling about – the man with the slicked-back hair who seemed to linger too long by the rare paintings, and the woman wearing an ill-fitting fur stole who kept glancing nervously at her watch.

"Jessie," George whispered, leaning towards her, "I have a feeling we're on the right track. Keep your eyes peeled for anything unusual."

"Right you are, George." Jessie's heart raced as she scanned the room.

In a quiet corner of the auction house, Jessie stumbled upon an animated conversation between two men. As she feigned interest in a nearby sculpture, snippets of their exchange floated to her ears.

"...the heist is planned for next week..."

"...won't know what hit 'em..."

"...we'll be long gone before they find out..."

Jessie's blood ran cold. Their discussion implied another heist was imminent. She had to share this information with George, but she knew that doing so would increase the danger they were in.

"George," Jessie said, her voice barely above a whisper as she sidled up to him, "I've just overheard something I think you need to know."

"Let's step outside," he suggested cautiously. Once they were clear of the crowd, Jessie relayed the conversation she had heard. George's expression darkened, and his grip tightened around his cane.

"Looks like we've got ourselves a lead to follow, Jessie. But we must tread carefully from now on. Our lives could very well depend on it."

"Agreed," Jessie replied, her determination unwavering. "If there's one thing I know for certain, it's that we owe it to Rosie and ourselves to see this through to the end."

"RING, RING." THE SHRILL sound of the telephone pierced the silence in Dale Street Private Investigations Agency office as Jessie sorted through papers on her desk.

"Jessie Harper speaking," she answered, her voice steady despite the sudden interruption.

"Ah, Miss Harper. How are your inquiries progressing?" The voice on the other end was smooth and menacing, sending a shiver down Jessie's spine.

"Who is this? What do you want?" Her heart hammered in her chest as she clutched the receiver tighter.

"Let's just say I'm someone who's taken an interest in your recent activities. You and Mr. Jenkins should tread lightly if you value your lives." With that, the line went dead. Jessie replaced the receiver with trembling hands, her face pale.

"Jessie, what's wrong?" George had entered the room, his eyes narrowed with concern as he took in her distressed demeanour.

"Someone called to warn us off, George. They used almost identical words to the previous threats. It's like they have trained someone to read from a script. They know we're getting close, and they don't like it." Jessie met George's gaze, fear flickering behind her steely determination.

"Then we'll be more careful, but we won't back down. We owe it to Rosie, remember?" George placed a comforting hand on Jessie's shoulder, a silent pledge of his unwavering support.

"Indeed, we do," Jessie agreed, taking a deep breath to calm her racing thoughts.

"Good evening, Jessie," Khan materialized beside her, his sleek black fur shimmering in the dim light. "I sense your unease. What has transpired?"

"Someone called, threatening our safety if we continue investigating," Jessie shared, stroking Khan's soft fur for comfort.

"Then I shall add a layer of magical protection around the office and the flat," Khan declared, his green eyes serious. "We must not let fear deter us from our pursuit of justice."

"Thank you, Khan," Jessie said, her gratitude evident. "We'll need all the help we can get."

"Speaking of which," George piped in, "I think it's time we reached out again to Detective Sergeant Bill Roberts. We could use some additional resources and support."

"Right you are, George," Jessie replied with renewed determination. "Let's arrange another meeting with Bill as soon as possible. The sooner we can expose this criminal syndicate and bring them to justice, the better."

With their course of action set, Jessie and George prepared for the next stage of their investigation, bolstered by the knowledge that they had loyal friends, both human and paranormal, ready to face the dangers that lay ahead.

BILL READILY AGREED to come to the office for the meeting. Waiting impatiently, Jessie's fingers tapped out a rhythm on the wooden desk, her eyes scanning the pages of a worn notebook filled with their gathered intelligence. Shadows danced over the room, as Khan flicked his tail, invisible to all but Jessie.

"Bill should be arriving any moment," George announced, breaking her concentration. He adjusted his tie and straightened his posture, anticipating the meeting ahead.

"Indeed," Jessie murmured, closing the notebook and tucking it safely into a drawer. A sudden knock at the door startled her, causing her heart to skip a beat.

"Right on time," George said, a hint of admiration in his voice as he opened the office door, revealing the bulk of Detective Sergeant Bill Roberts.

"Evening, George, Jessie," Bill greeted them, stepping inside the office. "I understand we have quite the situation on our hands."

"Thank you for coming, Bill," Jessie replied, gathering her thoughts. "As you know, we've uncovered a dangerous criminal syndicate, one that reaches far beyond Rosie O'Grady's murder."

"Quite so," George added. "And they're aware of our investigation, which has put all of us in peril."

"Then let's get to work," Bill said, determination etched onto his face. "What resources do you need from me?"

"First and foremost, we need information," Jessie explained, her mind racing with the possibilities. "We know there's a mastermind behind this whole operation, but we're still in the dark about their identity, although George has his suspicions."

"Leave that to me," Bill agreed, nodding solemnly. "I'll pull some strings within the force and see what I can find. I will make sure none of this gets back to the rotten apples."

"Moreover, if anything should happen to either of us..." Jessie hesitated for a moment before continuing, "We need someone on the inside who can carry on our mission."

"Consider it done, Jessie," Bill promised, his gaze unwavering. "You have my full support."

"Thank you, Bill," Jessie said, her voice thick with gratitude. She glanced over at George, who gave her a reassuring smile.

"Let's put an end to this syndicate once and for all," George declared, his cane tapping on the floor as he spoke as if celebrating with a victory jig.

"Agreed," Jessie echoed, feeling a mix of fear and determination coursing through her veins. She sensed Khan's presence at her side and knew that, together, they could face whatever challenges lay ahead.

As they delved into their plan of action, Jessie couldn't help but feel a sense of camaraderie between them, a bond forged by their shared desire for justice. The road ahead may be fraught with danger, but she knew they would not falter in their quest to bring the truth to light.

Chapter 31

JUST LIKE THE BOARD on the office wall, Jessie found herself constantly returning to the library and the adjacent art gallery in her quest to solve the riddles running through her mind. Her heart pounded in her chest as she quickened her pace, the sound of footsteps echoing behind her. This library visit had become a frantic race through shadowed streets. She dared not look back, lest she confirm the sinking suspicion that she was being followed. Jessie's mind raced with questions: Who could it be? What did they want? And most importantly, how had they discovered her whereabouts?

"Khan," she whispered urgently as she fumbled with her keys at the door of the office entrance, "I need your help."

In a flash, the black cat appeared at her side, his bright green eyes glinting with concern. "What is it, Jessie?" he asked.

"Someone's been following me." Jessie breathed heavily, her voice trembling. "I don't know who, but they must be connected to the syndicate."

"Take a deep breath, Jessie" Khan urged, his voice steady. "We'll find out who's behind this. But first, let me ensure our safety." With a flick of his tail, he weaved a magical layer of protection around the office – invisible to the human eye, but a formidable barrier against any would-be intruders.

"Thank you, Khan," Jessie said, relief washing over her as she stepped inside and locked the door.

"Remember," Khan reminded her, "our enemies are resourceful. We must remain vigilant and cautious."

"Indeed," Jessie agreed, her jaw set with determination. "But we cannot let fear dictate our actions. George and I will continue our investigation – we owe it to Rosie and everyone else whose lives have been shattered by this criminal enterprise."

"Very well," Khan replied, his eyes narrowing. "But I implore you, Jessie, please be careful."

"Of course," Jessie assured him, knowing that the stakes were higher than ever before. "We can't afford to let our guard down now."

THE FOLLOWING DAY, Jessie and George reconvened at the detective agency; their resolve unyielding despite the mounting dangers that beset them. As they concentrated over the latest leads and information, their minds whirred with theories and possibilities, each clue drawing them ever closer to the truth.

"Jessie," George said, his voice low and steady, "we must tread carefully. The syndicate is more powerful than we initially surmised. We cannot underestimate their reach or their ruthlessness."

"Agreed," she replied, her brow furrowed in thought. "But we cannot let fear hold us back. There are people counting on us, George – innocent lives at stake. To abandon our investigation now would be to forsake them all."

"Indeed," he conceded, his expression grim yet resolute. "We shall press on, then, as cautiously and diligently as possible. Together, Jessie, we will bring these criminals to justice and ensure that their reign of terror comes to an end."

"Here's to that," Jessie declared, her voice firm with conviction. Side by side, they delved deeper into the tangled web of deceit and danger that had ensnared them, their hearts buoyed by the hope that one day, the truth would finally come to light – and with it, the promise of justice for those who had suffered at the hands of the nefarious syndicate.

"GEORGE, WE OUGHT TO speak with Bill again to see if he has any news or information for us," Jessie suggested as they sat in their small but functional detective agency office. George nodded his agreement, and they wasted no time in contacting Detective Sergeant Bill Roberts.

"Jessie, George," Bill greeted them with a firm handshake when they met at the local police station. "I hope you are both well."

"Indeed, Bill, we are, but for how long?" Jessie replied, her tone serious. "You know there is a powerful syndicate involved in both Rosie O'Grady's murder and the art heist. We fear for our safety – and that of our friends."

Bill's eyes narrowed, concern etched on his face. "I understand the gravity of the situation. You have my full support and whatever resources I can provide. I have told you that before and nothing has changed,"

"Thank you, Bill. That means a great deal," George said, feeling a glimmer of hope amidst the growing darkness.

Jessie and George recounted the available intelligence on the syndicate. Hours of tireless effort led them to a suspicion that sent shivers down their spines – a name, whispered in hushed tones and cloaked in shadows, emerged as the mastermind behind the heist and murder.

"Yes, Rupert Thorne, my discreet inquiries have confirmed it is him," Bill revealed, his voice heavy with the weight of the knowledge. "A man of great wealth and influence, yet utterly ruthless."

"Thorne?" George echoed, his mind racing to comprehend the implications. "His reach extends far beyond anything we could have anticipated."

"Indeed," Jessie murmured, her thoughts turning inward as she considered the enormity of their task. "But now we know our enemy, and that gives us an advantage."

"True," Bill agreed. "But remember, Jessie, George, knowledge can be a double-edged sword. Be cautious in your pursuit – Thorne will not hesitate to eliminate anyone who threatens his empire."

"Understood, Bill," Jessie replied, her jaw set with determination. "George and I are prepared to face this challenge head-on, but we'll need your continued support."

"Of course," Bill assured them. "You have my word."

As the trio departed from their clandestine meeting, a palpable tension hung in the air, each of them acutely aware of the perilous path they now walked. But within that tension, there was also resolve – a shared commitment to exposing the truth and ensuring justice prevailed.

ON THEIR RETURN TO their office, both sleuths ruminated over all the events since the murder of Rosie O'Grady. "Jessie," George began, leaning over their cluttered office desk, "we need a plan to infiltrate Thorne's organization and bring him to justice."

"Agreed," Jessie said, her brow furrowed in thought. "We each have our unique skills, so let's utilize them. I can pose as an art collector interested in purchasing stolen works. That should get me close enough to gather information."

"Good idea." George traced his finger along the edge of a newspaper article detailing the last art heist in the city. "I'll work on finding vulnerabilities in his security. We know Thorne is always two steps ahead, so we must be cautious."

"Right," Jessie nodded, her determination unwavering. "We need to rely on our courage and tenacity, George. We've faced tough situations before, but this time, there's more at stake."

"We'll manage, Jessie. We always do," George replied with a reassuring smile.

THE DOCKLAND WAREHOUSE art gallery buzzed with activity as George and Jessie, now undercover again, mingled among the elite guests. They exchanged pleasantries and shared knowing glances, their thoughts focused on the mission at hand.

Yet amidst the glamour and intrigue, danger lurked in the shadows. Every movement was calculated, every word measured, as they navigated the treacherous web spun by Rupert Thorne.

George caught sight of a suspicious-looking man lurking near a side door - his keen instincts immediately aroused. With a subtle nod to Jessie, he slipped away from the crowd, following the stranger into a dimly lit corridor. He pressed himself against the wall, watching as the man entered a room marked 'Private.'

"Here's our chance," George murmured to himself, taking a steadying breath. He reached for the door handle, his heart pounding in his chest.

But as the door swung open, an iron grip seized George's arm, wrenching him into the room. His captors, Thorne's henchmen, sneered with cruel satisfaction.

"Look who we have here," one of them drawled, tightening his hold on George. "Thought you could outsmart us, didn't you? It will take more than a cripple to do that."

"Let me go," George demanded, struggling against the men's vice-like grip. "You won't get away with this."

"Are you sure about that?" another man taunted, his eyes glinting with malice.

MEANWHILE, JESSIE FELT a sudden shiver of unease, her instincts screaming for her to find George. As she made her way through the bustling crowd, she spotted the open door to the private room. She approached cautiously, her heart racing with dread.

From her hidden vantage point, Jessie witnessed George's capture and clenched her fists in anger. She knew she must act quickly, but carefully – any misstep could be disastrous. For a moment, she instinctively felt inside her bag for the gun but then remembered she had left it at the office owing to security measures at the gallery.

"Think, Jessie, think," she urged herself, her mind racing through countless scenarios. Time was running out, and she needed a plan – not just for herself, but for the friends she'd sworn to protect.

"Courage and tenacity," Jessie whispered, summoning her inner strength. With a deep breath, she slipped away from the gallery, determined to devise a strategy that would save George and bring down Rupert Thorne once and for all.

First stop, she used a telephone box to call Bill Roberts and told him to meet her at the agency as a matter of life and death.

Jessie hurried back to their detective agency, her footsteps echoing in the dimly lit street. She pushed open the door, her face flushed with urgency. "Khan, Bill – we have a serious problem," she announced, her voice wavering between panic and determination.

Khan materialized on the table, his green eyes narrowed with concern. "What's wrong, Jessie?"

"George has been captured by Thorne's henchmen. We must act quickly if we are to save him." Her words were met with a heavy silence as the gravity of the situation sank in.

"Captured?" Bill repeated, shaking his head in disbelief. "How did this happen?"

"Never mind that now," Jessie snapped, her patience thinning. "We need to come up with a plan to rescue him."

"All right, Jessie," Bill agreed, his tone resolute. "We'll do everything in our power to get George back safely. But first, we need to gather information and resources."

"Indeed," Khan chimed in, flicking his tail. "The more we know about Thorne's syndicate, the better our chances of rescuing George and bringing them down."

"Then let's not waste any more time," Jessie declared, her eyes shining with fierce resolve. They set to work, pooling their collective knowledge and calling in favours from trusted contacts. Each lead brought them closer to understanding the syndicate's inner workings, but the clock was ticking, and George's life hung in the balance.

"Brute force won't be enough," Jessie mused, pacing the floor. "We need something... unorthodox."

"Unorthodox?" Bill echoed, raising an eyebrow.

"Yes, out of the ordinary and I think I know what might work but Bill, you must swear never to reveal what you see or hear."

"As longs you don't want me to commit a crime, then I trust you. You have my word."

"Something they won't expect," Jessie clarified, her gaze drifting to Khan. An idea began to form, sparked by the supernatural abilities of her feline companion. "Khan, what if we used your powers to our advantage?"

Before Khan could react, Bill said, "Not the cat." Jessie smiled and nodded.

"Go on," Khan urged, his curiosity piqued.

"Your invisibility, for instance," she continued, her excitement growing. "We could use it to infiltrate their hideout undetected."

"An intriguing proposition," Khan conceded, his whiskers twitching thoughtfully. "But my powers alone may not be enough."

"Then we'll combine them with our own skills and resources," Jessie declared, her eyes alight with determination. "Together, we have a fighting chance at rescuing George and exposing Thorne's syndicate."

Bill nodded, impressed by Jessie's ingenuity. "It's a risky plan, but if there's even the slightest chance it could work, I'm in."

"Very well," Khan agreed, his voice steady. "Let us prepare for this daring undertaking."

As the trio set to work, refining their unconventional plan, Jessie couldn't help but feel a surge of gratitude for the unwavering loyalty of her friends. Their bond had been tested time and again, but they remained steadfast – a bulwark against the darkness that threatened to engulf them all.

"George," Jessie whispered, her heart swelling with determination. "We're coming for you, and we won't rest until you're safe."

Chapter 32

BOUND TO A RICKETY wooden chair in the faintly lit basement, George listened intently as the muffled voices of his captors drifted down from above. The musty scent of mould and damp earth permeated the air, but he forced himself to focus on their conversation, straining to catch every word.

"Thorne's got another job lined up," one man said, his voice heavy with greed. "A big one, too – worth more than all the others combined."

"Where's it happening?" another asked, the sound of clinking glass punctuating his curiosity.

"Can't say for sure. But I heard it involves an international shipment. A private collector's stash of rare relics."

George's heart pounded in his chest, his thoughts racing. This was the break they needed – a chance to put an end to Thorne's nefarious operation once and for all. But first, he had to find a way to relay this information to Jessie and Bill. If only there were some way to...

"Quiet!" Khan's voice, suddenly audible in George's mind, cut through his frenzied thoughts. "We're here. Are you ready?"

"Khan?" George whispered, stunned by the unexpected connection. "How did you...?"

"Jessie found a way to amplify my powers," the cat explained, his mental voice tinged with pride. "Now focus. We need to get you out of here."

"Right," George agreed, his determination renewed. He felt a sudden warmth envelop him, followed by a sensation akin to a gentle breeze brushing past his skin. The ropes binding him began to loosen, unravelling as if by an invisible hand.

"Bill is waiting just outside," Khan informed him, the confidence in his voice unmistakable. "Once you're free, we'll make our move."

"Understood," George replied, struggling to suppress his excitement as the last of his bonds fell away. He rose, wincing at the stiffness in his joints, and took a deep breath.

"Ready," he whispered, and at Khan's silent command, the door to the basement creaked open just a crack.

The sound of footsteps echoed from above, drawing nearer with each passing second. George's pulse quickened, but he steeled himself for the challenge ahead. This was it – their one chance to rescue him and gather the evidence they needed to bring Thorne's syndicate to its knees.

"Three... two... one..." Khan counted down, his presence a comforting anchor in the midst of danger.

"NOW!" George shouted, bursting through the door and limping up the stairs. He could sense Khan beside him, unseen but ever-present, guiding him through the chaos that erupted as their captors scrambled to respond.

Gunshots rang out, shattering the once-quiet evening, but George pressed on, fuelled by adrenaline and the knowledge that he held the key to dismantling Thorne's operation. As they neared the exit, he saw Bill, his familiar figure silhouetted against the night.

"Jessie! Khan! Bill!" George cried, relief washing over him as they converged outside. "I have information – about Thorne's next heist!"

"Excellent work, George," Jessie praised, her eyes shining with admiration and relief. "Now let's get you somewhere safe and plan our next move."

As they retreated into the darkness, George couldn't help but marvel at their unwavering loyalty and courage. The odds had been against them, but together, they'd defied them all, emerging stronger than ever. And with the crucial evidence now in their possession, they were one step closer to exposing the sinister truth behind Rosie O'Grady's murder and bringing Thorne's syndicate to justice.

WITHIN THE DIMLY LIT confines of the Dale Street Private Investigations Agency, Jessie, George, and Bill huddled around the table, their faces illuminated by the soft glow of a single lamp. Evidence lay strewn before them: documents, photographs, and scribbled notes. Tension hung in the air like an unbroken spider's web – delicate, yet resilient, with the promise of danger should it be disturbed.

"Here," Jessie said, her voice low and determined as she handed George a photograph. "This is our final connection."

George studied the image, his eyes narrowing at the sight of a familiar figure standing beside Rosie O'Grady. The man's smug expression sent a shiver down his spine, and he looked to Jessie for confirmation.

"Thorne," he muttered, clenching his fist.

"Indeed," Bill agreed, leaning in closer. "It seems Rosie O'Grady was involved with the syndicate after all. And from what you've uncovered, George, we now have enough evidence to tie Thorne and his organization to both the art heist and Rosie's murder."

Jessie's brow furrowed as she glanced between the two men. "We must tread carefully. With what we know now, any misstep could prove disastrous – not just for us, but for those caught in the syndicate's web."

"Agreed," George nodded, his gaze fixed on the photograph. He could almost feel Rosie's presence, urging him to seek justice for her untimely demise. "We must devise a strategy to expose them without alerting their suspicions."

"Let us consider the options," Bill suggested, his experience evident in the calm authority that underpinned his words. "We must strike swiftly and with precision, catching them off guard while ensuring that no innocents are harmed in the process."

"Indeed," Jessie concurred, her mind already racing with possibilities. "We must use our knowledge of Thorne's operations and the paranormal to our advantage, taking them by surprise."

"Perhaps," George mused, his eyes flicking between his companions, "we can possibly infiltrate one of their upcoming heists, gather irrefutable evidence against them, and bring the entire operation crashing down around Thorne's ears."

"Risky, but it may well be our best chance but it will need some meticulous planning and a large slice of luck," Bill admitted, nodding in approval.

Jessie's expression hardened, her resolve evident as she met both men's gazes. "Then it is settled. We shall prepare for our final confrontation, putting an end to Thorne's reign of terror once and for all."

"Let us proceed with caution, yet never lose sight of our objective," George added, his voice steady and resolute. "For Rosie, for justice, and for the countless souls ensnared in Thorne's web of deceit."

"Agreed," Jessie and Bill echoed in unison, their determination palpable as they set about crafting their plan – a plan that would usher in the climactic showdown, where darkness and light would collide with explosive force, and the truth would finally emerge victorious.

Chapter 33

JESSIE HARPER SURVEYED the room, her heart pounding as she prepared to unveil the truth. The remaining suspects gathered in the vicarage had come expecting answers, and she would not disappoint them. Her keen eye caught the various expressions that played across their faces: anticipation, fear, and even a hint of defiance.

"Thank you all for coming," Jessie began, keeping her tone steady despite the gravity of the situation. "We've assembled you here tonight to discuss the tragic murder of Rosie O'Grady. Through our investigation, we've uncovered connections that have led us to each of you."

Jessie's heart raced, her keen eyes darting from one suspect to the next. The room was charged with unease, each person offering a unique tapestry of emotions. George stood tall beside her, his cane tapping against the floor as he shifted his weight.

"Let us begin by addressing the matter of alibis," George said, his voice firm and authoritative. He turned to Beatrice Smythe. "You claimed to have had a premonition of Rosie's murder, yet your account of that night is elusive."

"Premonitions are not an exact science, Mr. Jenkins," Beatrice replied, her tone evasive. Jessie couldn't help but notice her fingers fidgeting with the lace hem of her dress, betraying her anxiety.

"Right," Jessie interjected, her voice sharp. "And what of you, Mr. Humphries? Your fascination with taxidermy is well-known, and your actions on the night of the murder remain shrouded in mystery."

Albert Humphries stiffened, his pale face flushing. "I've never harmed a living creature, Miss Harper. My interests lie solely in preserving beauty, not destroying it."

Jessie observed him closely, searching for any hint of deception. But even Khan, invisible to all but her, offered no clues as to whether the man spoke the truth.

"Moving on, then," George continued, directing his gaze at Geraldine Finch. "Your argument with Rosie on the evening of her death – care to explain?"

Geraldine's eyes flashed defensively. "It was nothing more than a heated exchange of words, I assure you. We had our differences, but I would never resort to murder."

Jessie and George exchanged glances, probing further. Geraldine's facade began to crack under the pressure, revealing hidden truths.

"Everyone in this room has secrets," Jessie declared, her voice firm. "Some of you have lied to us, while others have concealed important information. It is time for the truth to come to light."

"Indeed," George added, watching as the suspects shifted uncomfortably in their seats. "Particularly regarding Rosie's connection to the art heist and the shadowy syndicate that has been tailing us."

Whispers and gasps echoed through the room. Some, who knew Rosie well, denied any knowledge of such a connection, while others seemed to shrink into themselves, their silence speaking volumes.

"Allow me to remind you all of an anonymous threat we received during our investigation." George paused, scrutinizing each face for any flicker of recognition or guilt. "It seems someone in this very room wished for us to abandon our pursuit of the truth."

Jessie felt her resolve harden, her determination fuelled by the knowledge that one of these seemingly ordinary people had taken an innocent life. She turned to the vicar, fixing him with a pointed stare. "Reverend Bennett, it was your insistence on paranormal involvement that brought us here. Can you explain your eagerness to involve us in this matter?"

The vicar cleared his throat, his eyes darting between Jessie and George. "I-I simply sought to explore all avenues in the pursuit of justice for poor Rosie."

"Justice shall indeed be served," Jessie vowed, her voice resolute. "As we expose the secrets each of you harbours, we will reveal the true identity of Rosie's killer."

"Let us now turn our attention to the final suspects," George announced, his voice steady and unwavering. "Each of you presented with a motive and opportunity to commit this heinous crime."

Anticipation hung heavy in the air, the scent of fear and desperation mingling with the faint aroma of pipe smoke that clung to the room's furnishings. As Jessie and George prepared to unveil the murderer, every eye was fixed on them – and on each other.

"Based on our findings," George said, his voice firm and unyielding, "we can now reveal the identity of Rosie O'Grady's murderer."

"Speak up, then," the gardener at the back of the room snapped, his dirt-ingrained fingers tapping impatiently on the armrest of his chair. "The suspense is unbearable."

Jessie's gaze swept over the faces in the room, noting the beads of sweat that had formed on more than one brow. She could feel the weight of their anticipation, the gravity of the moment settling heavily upon them all.

"Very well," Jessie said, steeling herself for the revelation that would change everything. "The person responsible for Rosie O'Grady's murder is..."

The silence seemed to stretch on for an eternity, as though time itself held its breath in anticipation of the name that would fall from Jessie's lips.

"Albert Humphries," George declared, his voice ringing with authority and conviction.

A collective gasp echoed through the room, followed by a cacophony of exclamations, denials, and hushed whispers. Jessie watched as the reclusive taxidermist paled, the colour draining from his face like water down a drain.

"Th-this is preposterous," Albert stammered, his eyes wide with shock and disbelief. "I am innocent, I swear it!"

"Your fascination with taxidermy, your unusual behaviour during the night of the murder, and your connection to the art heist were all clues that led us to you," Jessie said, her voice unwavering. "But it was Khan who provided the final piece of the puzzle."

"Your cat?" Albert scoffed, his incredulity quickly giving way to anger. "You expect me to believe that your feline companion solved this case?"

"Believe what you will," Jessie replied, her expression resolute. "But Khan discovered a hidden compartment in your workshop – a compartment containing a bloodstained knife."

"Khan also found traces of the same rare poison used to stupefy Rosie in your possession," George added, his voice cold and unforgiving. "There can be no doubt that you, Albert Humphries, are the one who took her life."

"Enough!" Detective Sergeant Bill Roberts barked, rising from his chair with a scowl etched upon his face. "I've heard all I need to make an arrest. Mr. Humphries, you're under suspicion for the murder of Rosie O'Grady. You'll be coming with me to the station."

Jessie watched as Albert was led away in handcuffs, the room still abuzz with shock and disbelief. As the reality of their discovery settled in, she felt a strange mixture of relief and sadness – relief that justice would be served, but also sadness for the life that had been so cruelly snuffed out.

"Jessie," George said quietly, placing a hand on her shoulder. "We did it. We found Rosie's killer."

"Indeed, we did," Jessie replied, her voice sombre. "But let us not forget that our work is far from over. We must remain vigilant, for there are more mysteries to solve and more lives to save."

As the local uniformed constables arrived to take custody of Albert Humphries, Jessie, George, Bill Roberts and Khan shared a quiet moment of victory. Their first major case had been solved, but they knew that it was just the beginning of their journey together. And as they looked around the room at the faces of those whose secrets had been laid bare, they understood that in the world of crime, nothing was ever truly as it seemed.

Chapter 34

JESSIE STOOD IN THE middle of the office, her auburn hair casting shadows on her pale face as she struggled to comprehend the enormity of the events since Rosie was killed. George leaned heavily upon his cane, his jaw clenched tight in an attempt to steady himself.

Moving over to her desk, Jessie's fingers traced the edge of the worn, leather-bound notebook as she glanced at George. His furrowed brow and clenched jaw betrayed his inner turmoil. She knew they were both grappling with the horrifying revelation of the killer's identity, but there was no turning back now.

"George," Jessie began tentatively, "we've come so far in this investigation. We can't let doubt cloud our judgement now."

"Of course not," George replied, though his voice faltered ever so slightly. "It's just... How could someone we thought we knew turn out to be such a monster?"

Jessie sighed, her thoughts drifting to Rosie – her vibrant spirit snuffed out by a callous hand. A wave of sadness washed over her, followed closely by anger at the senselessness of it all.

"Sometimes people hide their true selves behind a mask," she said quietly. "We must remember that we're doing this for Rosie. She deserves justice."

"Absolutely," George agreed, determination flickering in his eyes. "I just wish I could shake this feeling of... helplessness."

"None of this is your fault, George," Jessie reassured him, placing a hand on his shoulder. "We'll get through this together."

As if sensing their distress, Khan materialized beside them, his bright green eyes gleaming with concern. The enigmatic cat offered silent comfort, a solid presence amid the emotional storm raging all around them.

"Jessie, do you truly believe justice will be served?" George asked hesitantly, voicing the doubts that plagued them both.

"Justice isn't perfect, but we have to have faith in the system," Jessie replied, though she shared his concerns about potential loopholes. "Our responsibility is to honour Rosie's memory by doing everything in our power to ensure her killer doesn't escape punishment."

"Right you are," George said with renewed resolve. "We've faced many obstacles so far, but we've also shown that we're a force to be reckoned with."

"Indeed," Jessie agreed, the corners of her mouth lifting in a small smile as she recalled their past successes. "And we've come too far to back down now."

"Then let's continue our pursuit of the truth," George declared, taking Jessie's hand and giving it a reassuring squeeze.

"Agreed," Jessie said, her determination bolstered by George's unwavering support.

The pair stood together, drawing strength from one another as they prepared for the challenges that awaited them – the dangerous syndicate they had antagonized, the threat to their own lives, and the personal losses they had endured. Though doubt still lingered, Jessie and George knew that their journey was only just beginning, and their commitment to uncovering the truth would see them through to the end.

As Jessie looked upon the rows of leather-bound books lining the vicarage walls, her thoughts wandered to Rosie O'Grady, a woman whose life had been snuffed out with brutal senselessness. She felt a pang of guilt and the weight of responsibility heavy on her shoulders.

"George," she said quietly, "do you ever wonder if we've done right by Rosie? I mean, have our efforts thus far truly honoured her?"

George's gaze followed Jessie's as he considered her words, his expression sombre. "I can't say for certain, but one thing I do know is that we've given it our all. We're not finished yet, Jessie."

"Perhaps," Jessie conceded, though doubt still gnawed at her. "But what if our involvement has only made things worse? What if we've put ourselves and others in danger?"

"Jessie, we couldn't have known the full extent of what we were getting into," George replied, his voice firm. "We mustn't let fear paralyze us now."

"Easy for you to say," Jessie countered, frustration bubbling up within her. "You weren't the one who insisted on taking this case in the first place!"

"Nor was I the one who backed down when things got difficult," George reminded her gently. "Jessie, we've faced obstacles before, and we've always come through. I believe we can do it again."

"Even when the stakes are so much higher?" Jessie questioned, her voice barely above a whisper.

"Especially then," George said, meeting her eyes with unwavering determination. "Together, we can overcome anything."

It was then that Khan emerged from the shadows, his green eyes gleaming with concern. He wound himself around Jessie's legs, offering a comforting purr.

"Thank you, Khan," Jessie murmured, bending down to stroke his sleek black fur. She felt a sense of solace in his presence, and her spirits lifted ever so slightly.

"Jessie," George began, his voice hesitant but resolute, "I promise you, we will find the truth and ensure that justice is served, no matter what it takes."

"Even if it costs us everything?" Jessie asked, her eyes searching George's for reassurance.

"Even then," George confirmed, his resolve unshaken.

"Very well," Jessie conceded, torn between the desire for justice and the fear of the unknown. She knew, though, that there could be no turning back now. Their journey had only just begun.

"Then let's plan our next steps," she declared, her mind shifting from despair to determination. Together, they would face whatever lay ahead, their friendship and partnership stronger than ever. And as they exchanged glances, an unspoken understanding passed between them - the bonds they shared were not merely those of camaraderie, but something deeper, more profound.

"Agreed," George said, his eyes reflecting the same newfound realization. "We'll forge ahead, come what may."

With renewed purpose, Jessie and George began to strategize their course of action, the shadows of doubt receding as their resolve solidified. And as they pledged themselves to the pursuit of justice, they found comfort in each other's strength, their commitment unwavering even in the darkest hour.

The room seemed to shrink around them, the walls closing in as Jessie and George stared at each other, their faces pale with the weight of the revelation. The killer's identity gnawed at their minds, a sickening truth that threatened to overwhelm them.

"Can you believe it?" Jessie stammered, her voice barely a whisper. She felt as though she'd been plunged into an icy abyss, her thoughts scattered and disjointed.

"Absolutely not," George replied, his jaw tight with tension. "But there it is, staring us in the face."

Jessie paced back and forth, her heels clicking on the wooden floor, the sound echoing through the room like a ticking clock. Her mind raced as she tried to piece together the implications of this latest development.

"Jessie, we must remain calm," George said, his voice steady despite the turmoil within him. He rubbed the back of his neck, attempting to alleviate the tension that had settled there. "We need to consider our next move carefully. If we act rashly, we risk putting ourselves in even more danger."

Jessie stopped pacing, her brow furrowed as she considered George's words. "You're right," she conceded, her voice firming with resolve. "But we cannot let this discovery paralyze us. We have a duty to Rosie, and to every other innocent soul who has been affected by this heinous crime."

She met George's gaze, her eyes shining with determination, and saw her own conviction mirrored there. They were both resolute in their pursuit of justice, no matter how treacherous the path before them.

"Indeed," George agreed, his hand absently reaching for the pipe on the table beside him. "But we must also protect ourselves, Jessie. We have stumbled upon something much larger and more dangerous than we had anticipated."

Jessie nodded, her thoughts turning inward. She knew George was right - they needed to tread carefully to avoid the snares that surely lay ahead. But beneath her fear and apprehension, a fire burned within her - a fierce, unyielding desire to expose the truth and bring the killer to justice.

"Very well," she said at last, steeling herself for the challenges that awaited them. "Let us proceed with caution but let us also remember our purpose. We have come too far to falter now."

"Agreed," George replied, his expression resolute. "Together, we will see this through to the end."

"It's time to go and see Reverend Bennett now he is no longer a suspect," Bill said.

IN THE QUIET, DIMLY lit vicarage, Jessie's gaze absently traced the worn patterns of the Persian rug beneath her feet. She could sense George's presence beside her, a comforting warmth in the midst of their shared sorrow. The grandfather clock by the door ticked away the seconds, each one heavy with regret and grief for the vibrant woman who had been ripped from this world so violently.

"Rosie was a force of nature," Jessie murmured, her voice barely louder than the whispering wind outside. "She deserved better than this - than being reduced to another crime statistic."

"Indeed, she did," George replied softly, his eyes downcast. "Her laughter could light up a room, and she had such a zest for life despite her difficult circumstances. It's hard to believe that someone could snuff out that flame so callously."

Jessie could feel the weight of Rosie's memory pressing down upon them, a tangible reminder of the injustice they sought to rectify. As she closed her eyes, the image of Rosie's wild red hair and fiery spirit leapt into her mind, undimmed by the passage of time. "We were supposed to protect her," she whispered, anguish lacing her words.

"Jessie, we mustn't blame ourselves," George said gently, placing a hand on her shoulder. "We couldn't have known what would happen. All we can do now is ensure that her killer does not escape justice."

"Justice," Jessie echoed, bitterness tinging the word. She opened her eyes and stared at the flickering candlelight, shadows dancing across the walls like ghostly figures. "Is there truly any justice for people like Rosie? Or are we just chasing after shadows?"

"Perhaps," George conceded, his voice solemn. "But we cannot allow that thought to paralyze us. We have a duty to pursue the truth, wherever it may lead."

"Even if it leads us into darkness?" Jessie asked, her gaze searching George's face for reassurance.

"Especially then," George replied firmly. "For it is in the darkest corners that the truth often hides. What do you think, Reverend Bennett?"

The priest shrugged. He was content to let George and Jessie talk and reminisce about Rosie.

Jessie took a deep breath, drawing strength from George's conviction. As they stood together in the stillness of the vicarage, she knew they were bound by more than just friendship; they shared a fierce determination to right the wrongs inflicted upon Rosie and others like her. And though the path ahead seemed fraught with danger, she could not imagine turning back now. A sense of resolve settled over her as she nodded in agreement. "Very well, then. We will continue our quest for justice, no matter what challenges we face. For Rosie, and for ourselves."

"Indeed," George echoed, his voice steady and unwavering. "Together, we will make certain that her memory remains alive and her spirit honoured."

In that moment, as the heaviness of their hearts was tempered by their unyielding commitment, Jessie knew that they had taken the first step toward healing – not only for themselves but for the world that Rosie had left behind. And as they turned their thoughts to the future and the battles yet to be fought, they did so with the knowledge that they would face whatever came next side by side.

Chapter 35

"GEORGE, I THINK IT'S time we put the pieces together." Jessie Harper stood in the centre of Dale Street Private Investigations Agency. Her auburn hair pulled back into a tight bun. Her eyes were focussed and determined as she scanned the room, taking in the extensive notes they'd made during the investigation.

"Quite right, Jessie," George replied, limping toward his desk chair. He leaned on his cane, carefully lowering himself into the seat before riffling through their compiled documents. "We've got a solid case, but we need to align our findings to make sure Bill and his bosses are on board with the case."

"Indeed," Jessie murmured, turning her attention to Khan. The sleek black cat sat perched on the edge of the desk, his green eyes alert and watchful. "Khan, would you mind sharing your observations? Your unique perspective might reveal something we've missed."

"Of course, Jessie," Khan replied, his voice low and measured. "May I say it's such a relief now George knows all about me. Bill too, for that matter." He recounted his insights, Jessie listened intently, nodding occasionally as if to confirm connections that were forming in her mind.

Hours passed as Jessie, George, and Khan dissected the case, sifting through layers of information in search of the elusive thread that would bind everything together. They discussed the garden party, the murder, and the stolen art, their conversation punctuated by the ticking of the office clock.

"Wait a moment," Jessie said suddenly, her brow furrowing. "We're missing something. One more piece of evidence... Something that will solidify our case."

"Back to the vicarage garden then?" George suggested, setting aside the papers with a sigh.

"Exactly," Jessie agreed, determination etching itself across her features.

"Very well. Let us depart without delay." With that, the three investigators set off for the scene of the crime, their hearts heavy with the knowledge that time was running short.

UPON ARRIVING AT THE vicarage, Jessie, George, and Khan wasted no time in scouring the area. They searched every corner of the main and the walled gardens, their keen senses attuned to any overlooked clue. It wasn't long before Jessie stumbled upon a sharp glint in the shadows – a discarded jewellery piece that matched the description of a stolen item from the infamous art heist.

"George, look at this!" Jessie exclaimed, holding up the piece triumphantly. "This could be the missing link we've been searching for."

"Indeed, it could," George agreed, his eyes narrowing as he examined the find. "It's time for us to confront our killer."

"Let's gather the remaining suspects and other interested parties at the vicarage," Jessie suggested. "We'll reveal our findings under the guise of new information about Rosie's murder."

"An excellent plan," George concurred. "The truth will out, and justice will be served."

As those summoned or invited began arriving at the vicarage, the atmosphere grew thick with tension. Jessie, George, and Khan exchanged determined glances, each silently reaffirming their shared goal: unveiling the truth and securing justice for Rosie O'Grady.

"Thank you for joining us this evening," Jessie began, her voice steady as she addressed the assembled crowd. "We have some important information to share regarding Rosie's murder."

"Go on, then," Reverend Bennett interjected, scepticism dripping from his words.

"Very well," George replied, unfazed by the vicar's derision. He and Jessie proceeded to narrate the events of Rosie's murder as they'd pieced them together, revealing the connection to the art heist.

"Impossible!" Eleanor Foster, the local schoolteacher, gasped, her haughty façade crumbling as she clutched her pearls.

"Hardly," Jessie countered, her gaze unrelenting as she and George systematically dismantled alibis and presented solid evidence to disprove lies. "The truth has a way of emerging, despite our best efforts to keep it buried."

"Indeed," George added, his voice heavy with the weight of their revelations. "And now, we present to you the final piece of evidence linking Rosie's murder to the art heist." He gestured toward Jessie, who held aloft the discarded jewellery piece.

"Behold," she declared, her eyes locked on Geraldine Finch. "You thought your secret was safe, but justice cannot be denied. We accuse you, Geraldine, of taking Rosie O'Grady's life for your own gain."

"Preposterous!" Geraldine sputtered; her face flushed with indignation. She attempted to flee, but Khan, invisible to all but Jessie and George, tripped her up, allowing George and others to apprehend her.

Jessie's heart raced as she and George stood before the apprehended Geraldine Finch, her eyes darting around the room like a caged animal. The smug confidence she had displayed earlier was gone, replaced with an expression of desperation.

"Explain yourselves!" Geraldine demanded, her voice cracking under the weight of the accusations. "What evidence do you possibly have to support these preposterous claims?"

"Very well," George declared, his voice steely and resolute. He produced a sheaf of papers, which he handed over to Jessie. "Shall we begin with the art heist, Geraldine?"

"Art heist?" Several surprised murmurs rippled through the gathered crowd.

"Indeed," Jessie confirmed, her gaze never leaving Geraldine's face. "You see, Geraldine, we believe that Rosie O'Grady stumbled upon your plan to steal a collection of priceless artifacts. I say your plan, but you were a mere pawn in the grip of a powerful crime syndicate. And when she threatened to expose you, you silenced her in the most brutal way imaginable. It was no excuse that you were acting under instructions. "

"Preposterous!" Geraldine spat, her face flushed with anger. "I know nothing of any art heist!"

"Ah, but you do," George interjected with a sly smile. "You see, we found a piece of jewellery at the vicarage garden - one that matches the description of a stolen item from said heist."

Jessie held up the gold necklace, its jewelled pendant gleaming in the light. The attentive crowd gasped, their attention now fully on the damning evidence.

"Your lies won't save you now, Geraldine," Jessie stated flatly, her heart pounding in her chest. "We have more than enough evidence to prove your guilt."

Geraldine's eyes flickered between Jessie and George, the fear in her eyes betraying her crumbling facade. "You...you can't prove anything," she stammered, her voice barely above a whisper.

"Actually, we can," Jessie replied, her tone firm. "We have witnesses who can testify to your movements on the night of Rosie's murder. And let us not forget the stolen artifacts found in your possession."

"Now I know you are bluffing," Geraldine said.

Just then, Bill Roberts appeared in the doorway, his expression grim. "Is she?" Bill said, holding up a priceless miniature painting, "this artwork and other stolen artifacts were found in your room not less than an hour ago."

"Enough!" Geraldine shrieked, lunging for the necklace in Jessie's hand. But Khan, ever vigilant, flicked his tail and tripped her once more, sending her crashing to the ground.

"Seems you've run out of options, Geraldine," George observed coolly as Jessie moved to retrieve the fallen necklace. "The game is up."

"Your actions have caused great pain and suffering to those around you," Jessie declared, her voice heavy with emotion. "And while we cannot bring Rosie back, we can ensure that justice is served."

"Geraldine Finch, I am placing you under arrest for the murder of Rosie O'Grady and your involvement in the art heist." Detective Sergeant Roberts said.

"Enough of this charade!" Geraldine spat, "You have your killer. Humphries was arrested."

"You mean me? If so, yes, I am part of the charade."

All eyes and necks swivelled towards the back of the room where a smiling Albert Humphries raised his hands to demonstrate he was not handcuffed and thus a free man. Detective Sergeant Bill Roberts was now standing next to him trying hard to wipe a smug look from his face for he was also a part of this subterfuge.

"Justice must prevail," Jessie asserted, her voice impassioned as she delivered a speech about the value of a single life and the importance of accountability. "No matter how high the stakes, we will not stand idly by while evil goes unchecked."

"Take her away," Bill Roberts commanded.

With Geraldine in police custody, Jessie, George, and Khan finally allowed themselves a sigh of relief. They'd solved their first major case together – a testament to their skill and determination.

Two uniformed constables moved forward to apprehend the now sobbing woman, while Jessie, George, and Khan shared a solemn moment of silent triumph. They had done it - they had solved their first major case together and brought justice to Rosie.

As Jessie watched Geraldine being led away, she couldn't help but feel a sense of satisfaction mixed with sorrow. They had uncovered the truth, but at what cost? The lives of those involved would never be the same.

But as she glanced at George and Khan, she knew one thing for certain: this wouldn't be their last adventure. Their journey as detectives had only just begun.

"Quite the journey we've had," Jessie mused, her gaze distant as she reflected on the harrowing events that had brought them to this moment. "But I can't help feeling that this is just the beginning of our detective adventures."

"Indeed," George agreed, a smile tugging at his lips. "I believe our partnership is destined for great things."

"Agreed," Khan chimed in, his eyes gleaming with anticipation. "The three of us make quite the formidable team."

Epilogue

"AH, JESSIE, GEORGE," Detective Sergeant Bill Roberts said as they entered Liverpool's Hatton Garden police station, the killer having been deposited in the cells of the nearby Main Bridewell. "You've done it, Brilliant work."

"Thank you, Detective Sergeant," Jessie replied, her auburn hair catching the light as she handed over the evidence that sealed the killer's fate. "We couldn't have done it without your guidance and help."

"Indeed," George chimed in, his cane tapping on the tiled floor as he walked beside Jessie. "We're glad we could bring the murderer to justice."

"Justice will be served, I assure you," Roberts promised.

"To a degree, but Thorne was behind all of this and gets off scot-free," Jessie remarked.

"Tell me, Bill, your informant was the key to cracking this case wide open. It was he or she that knew all about the secret society. Will they be safe from the likes of Thorne?"

"Very safe. For obvious reasons I can't explain why I say that. Just trust me. I must say this though, it was my informant, but it was you two who brilliantly engineered the smokescreen of linking suspects to the secret society and using Albert Humphries as a false suspect. The real brilliance was that the secret society really existed. That really must have made Geraldine Finch, and the syndicate drop their respective guards."

Jessie and George nodded as they knew Bill was right but Jessie once more repeated her regrets that Thorne had escaped justice.

Bill Roberts and George knew she was right and decided to say nothing.

As word of the killer's capture spread throughout Liverpool and the village of Old Swan in particular, the citizens breathed easier, knowing the danger had passed. Jessie and George felt a sense of relief, their efforts not in vain.

AS THEY RETURNED TO the vicarage, Reverend Albert Bennett greeted them warmly. "Thank you both so much for your diligent work and bravery. Our village and the larger community can begin healing now."

"Thank you, Reverend," Jessie said, her heart warmed by his gratitude. "We're just glad we could help."

"Indeed," George added, his gaze steady. "We'll continue to do everything we can to ensure the safety of this community."

"There are also two young ladies here waiting to speak to you, Jessie." Reverend Bennett said.

Ellen and Joyce O'Grady spoke shyly and as one voice, "Hello Miss Harper."

"Please, Jessie to you two and I think you know why."

"That's one of the things we wanted to tell you apart from thanking you for bringing our mother's killer to justice," The elder sister, Ellen said.

Joyce continued, "This is hard, but we must tell you that our mother is not your mother."

"What? Why?" Jessie said.

"I spotted it. The third sister in the photograph has a finger missing from her right hand. That was Amelda and she went missing and never found. It's not you like you thought. I am sorry because we would love you to be our sister," Ellen said looking teary-eyed.

"You are my sisters at least in spirit and you can come and see me any time you wish," Jessie said.

"GEORGE," JESSIE MUSED later that evening. "I think we should continue our detective agency. There will always be mysteries to solve, and together, I believe we can make a difference."

"Jessie, I couldn't agree more," he replied, a spark of excitement in his eyes, "and we can also set about tracing your mother if that is your desire."

"That can wait. Let us always remember the lessons we've learned from this case," Jessie proposed. "Justice is not easy, but it's always worth fighting for."

"Absolutely," George concurred. "And I know we have a bright future ahead of us."

As they settled into their routine at Dale Street Private Investigations Agency, they now felt confident enough in the agency future to employ Isabel as a receptionist. Jessie felt a newfound sense of purpose and determination. With Khan by her side and George as her partner, they were ready to tackle whatever new adventures awaited them.

Jessie couldn't help but marvel at how far she had come from her quiet life as a librarian. She felt a sense of fulfilment in helping solve the mystery and aiding her community. It was a feeling she hadn't known she craved until now.

As news of the killer's capture spread throughout Liverpool, a palpable sense of relief washed over the city. The community breathed easier knowing the danger had passed, and Jessie could see the gratitude etched on the faces of their neighbours.

"LET'S PAY OUR RESPECTS to Rosie," Jessie suggested, her voice softened with reverence. George nodded in agreement, and the pair made their way through the cemetery to the freshly dug grave marking the resting place of Rosie O'Grady.

Jessie clutched a small bouquet of wildflowers in her hands, a humble tribute to a woman who had faced life's hardships with resilience and grace. They stood side by side at the foot of the grave, a sombre silence settling over them as the reality of Rosie's fate weighed heavy on their hearts.

"Rosie," Jessie murmured, laying the flowers gently on the grave. "We did it. Your killer has been caught."

George removed his hat and bowed his head. "Justice has been done, and we promise you, it won't be forgotten."

A quiet moment passed, and Jessie felt the air around them shift subtly, as if Rosie's spirit had acknowledged their words. The once-stifling atmosphere seemed to lift, replaced by a sense of closure and peace.

"Quite a journey, eh?" George remarked, breaking the silence. He glanced at Jessie, whose eyes were still fixed on the grave. "You've been extraordinary throughout all this, you know."

"Thank you, George," she replied, turning to face him. "But I couldn't have done it without you. We make quite a team."

"Indeed," he agreed, a tender smile playing at the corners of his lips. "The bond we've forged, the trust we've built... it's what brought us here, to the end of this case."

"Or perhaps," Jessie mused, her eyes flicking up to meet his, "it's just the beginning."

"Beginning, you say?" George asked, cocking an eyebrow curiously. Jessie could see the faintest hint of a blush creeping up his cheeks.

"Of our partnership," she clarified, her heart swelling with affection. "We've proven ourselves capable of so much together. Who knows what other mysteries await us?"

"Ah, yes," George chuckled softly, his eyes twinkling with warmth. "I can't think of anyone else I'd rather face those challenges with."

"Nor I," Jessie agreed, her words laced with sincerity.

They shared a lingering look, the connection between them stronger than ever before. In the depths of each other's eyes, they saw not only the triumph of justice served but also the promise of a future filled with camaraderie and adventure.

"Shall we then, partner?" George asked, offering his arm to Jessie with a gentlemanly bow.

"Indeed," she replied, taking his arm with a grin. "Onward, to whatever awaits us."

As they walked away from Rosie's grave, leaving behind the past and its sorrows, an unspoken love stirred in the air around them – a testament to the strength of their bond and the unwavering partnership that had been forged amidst the chaos.

"HERE'S TO NEW BEGINNINGS, Miss Harper," George murmured, raising a glass of beer in toast while they took in the surroundings of the newly opened Ship & Mitre public house in Dale Street. The place bustled with life and energy, a stark contrast from the sombre cemetery they had just left.

Jessie smiled and raised her own beer glass. "Indeed, Mr. Jenkins. To new beginnings." As she spoke, a surge of pride welled up within her. She marvelled at how far she had come from her quiet life as a librarian. There was something immensely satisfying about knowing she had played a crucial role in unravelling the mystery and helping her community find peace.

ONCE THEY HAD RETIRED to the office, Jessie saw her cat under the desk. She sensed he was feeling a bit left out of the celebrations.

"Khan, come here, old chap," Jessie called softly to the black cat. The feline appeared from under the desk, his bright green eyes gleaming with otherworldly wisdom. He flicked his tail, pleased by the attention.

"Jessie, I believe our friend Khan deserves a treat for his indispensable assistance during this investigation," George suggested, admiration evident in his voice.

"Indeed, he does," Jessie agreed as she offered Khan a small piece of fish. The cat purred contentedly, accepting the reward with grace.

"Wait, is this red herring?" Khan said at the same time as a grin wider than the Mersey Tunnel spread from one feline ear to the other.

Gradually, the laughter subsided, and it was George who broke the silence. "Jessie, you've come so far from your quiet life as a librarian," he observed thoughtfully. "You should feel proud of what you've accomplished."

She considered his words, realizing that he was right. The satisfaction she felt from solving the mystery and protecting her community was undeniable. She had found her calling, and she embraced it wholeheartedly.

"Jessie, do you know what I've realized?" George asked her "Our partnership, our combined skills – we've created something truly powerful. And I admire your courage and dedication more than I can say."

"Thank you, George," Jessie responded sincerely. "I'm grateful to have you by my side."

"Miss Harper, Mr. Jenkins, a letter for you," Isabel, the new receptionist, announced, entering the office with an envelope in hand. Jessie took it, noting the official seal of the Liverpool City Police.

"Detective Sergeant Bill Roberts sent us a formal thank you for our work on the case," she shared as she read the letter. "He hopes we can collaborate again in the future."

"Ah, recognition from the authorities," George mused. "Seems we are making quite an impression."

"Indeed," Jessie smiled. "But let's not forget our true purpose – justice and the pursuit of truth. That includes bringing down Rupert Thorne at the first opportunity we have."

"Agreed," George concurred. "We shall remain vigilant, always ready to face new challenges."

With that resolution in mind, Jessie Harper and George Jenkins closed the chapter on the Rosie O'Grady case, looking forward to whatever adventures awaited them in their cozy corner of Liverpool. And as they continued their detective work, they knew they were not just surviving, but truly living.

As days passed, Liverpool began to heal, with people sharing stories of Rosie O'Grady's vibrant personality. Her memory lived on, a testament to the indomitable spirit of those who refused to be silenced.

A sense of calm settled over the sleuths and their mysterious cat. Their work here was done... for now.

CONFIDENTIAL POLICE NOTES

REGARDING THE INVESTIGATION of the murder of Rosie O'Grady and the associated art theft from the Walker Art Gallery:

- The occult secret society did exist, but JH & GJ* with DS Roberts used it as a smokescreen once they knew Rosie, Rupert Thorne**, and Gerladine Finch all connected to the heist and the murder. * Initials used to protect identities ** Still at large and suspected of being the head of a major crime syndicate.
- There was no blood at the crime scene as Geraldine Finch stabbed Rosie O'Grady to death beforehand and had help moving the body to the vicarage garden. It is believed her lover, a young man recently released from jail, moved the body but in interview he denied all allegations so remains free. He and Finch placed the so-called supernatural signs such as the feather, claw marks, and symbols.
- Finch told investigators about the map and the relic hidden in the church to ingratiate herself with the investigators. She knew of them as a member of the occult secret society.
- There was no evidence that the Reverend Bennett was a member of the secret society or engaged in the dark arts.
- Constable Walker who impersonated a police officer was believed to be Rupert Thorne but there is no proof of that.
- Vanishing sisters of Rosie O'Grady remains a mystery.

About the Author

KJ CORNWALL[1] is the pen name of multi-genre author Stephen Bentley[2], a former British detective and barrister. It is the name associated with the Jessie Harper Paranormal Cozy Mystery series with 'Murder at the Vicarage' as the first book in the series.

The series is set in 1930s Liverpool, a city the author knows well.

Why KJ Cornwall? The memories of Kathleen, the author's mother and Jack. her twin brother, are cherished by the author in the choice of this pen name.

The signup page for KJ's mailing list is here for news of new releases in the Jessie Harper Paranormal Cozy Mystery series.[3]

1. https://books.kjcornwall.com/

2. https://books.stephenbentley.info/

3.   https://books.kjcornwall.com/

Did you love *Murder at the Vicarage: A Jessie Harper Paranormal Cozy Mystery*? Then you should read *Jessie Harper Meets Khan the Talking Cat* by KJ Cornwall!

This free (for subscribers) introduction to the Jessie Harper paranormal cozy mystery series tells the story of how Jessie Harper, our protagonist, met her talking cat, Khan, her sidekick. It's set in 1930s Liverpool, England, where Jessie works as a librarian in the city's largest reference library. She specializes in books about the supernatural world. This introductory offer is designed to tempt you to read more about Jessie and her friends including Khan. The series will be clean and cozy with only a dash of paranormal, and that's Khan. There will be no witches nor tales of the occult. KJ and Khan hope you will support the series, and of course enjoy it.

<u>Get it here!</u>[4]

Finally, Khan and KJ would be delighted if you left a review at the store where you bought this book. A few words will suffice.

---

4.   https://books.kjcornwall.com/

Don't miss out!

Visit the website below and you can sign up to receive emails whenever KJ Cornwall publishes a new book. There's no charge and no obligation.

https://books2read.com/r/B-A-TEYX-AJYHC

BOOKS 2 READ

Connecting independent readers to independent writers.

Milton Keynes UK
Ingram Content Group UK Ltd.
UKHW040723290823
427678UK00001B/89